This  _____

Children's
POOLBEG

book belongs to

ELF IN THE HEAD

DIE IN THE HEAD

Christine Nöstlinger
ELF in the HEAD

With illustrations by Jutta Bauer

TRANSLATED BY SEAN McMAHON

Children's
POOLBEG

Der Zwerg im Kopf
translated from the German as *Elf in the Head* by Sean McMahon

© Beltz Verlag, Weinheim and Basel 1989
Programm Beltz und Gelberg, Weinheim
Alle Rechte vorbehalten

© Translation Sean McMahon 1992

This English-language version published 1992 by
Poolbeg Press Ltd
Knocksedan House,
Swords, Co Dublin, Ireland

ISBN 1 85371 213 2

Cover and inside illustrations by Jutta Bauer
Cover design by Pomphrey Associates
Typeset by Mac Book Limited in ITC Stone 10/14
Printed by The Guernsey Press Company Ltd
Vale, Guernsey, Channel Islands

Contents

1
The Coming of the Elf

Anna had the elf in her head for some time. One night a couple of days after her sixth birthday it happened. She was standing yawning beside her bed and was about to pull back the flowered quilt when she saw the elf. He was sitting on a pink rose and he was tiny! Even if you included his violet pointy cap he was still smaller than the nail of Anna's little finger. And he had such a faint voice—so light that she could not make out what he was saying until, holding him between her thumb and index finger, she put him to her ear. Then she heard him complaining, "Stop, blast you! You're squashing me flat."

So she sat him on the edge of her ear but that did not please him either. He complained, "Are you joking? Don't you know I have vertigo?" In sheer terror that he might fall and smash himself to bits he dug his finger right in Anna's ear. That hurt so much that Anna screeched and shook her head like mad to try to dislodge him but all she did was to drive him further into the ear. Right inside! And in doing so he lost his pointy cap. Anna pulled and pulled at it, screaming all the while, until it was out, but she could not get a grip on the elf.

She ran into the living-room to her papa. He was sitting on the sofa darning one of Anna's red socks which had a big hole at the heel.

"Papa, I have an elf in my head!" she wailed. "Get him out for me."

Her papa laid aside the stocking and the darning-needle and laughed.

"It's the truth!" yelled Anna and began hitting her left ear.

"That's great!" said he, laughing all the more. "An elf in the head is a splendid thing to have. From now on he can tell you your bedtime story. An elf is bound to be better than me." He didn't believe her. He thought that the story of the elf in the head was just another of the tricks she regularly played so as not to go to bed when she was told.

"You're just being stupid," cried Anna in desperation. She lifted the sewing-basket and took out a crochet hook, intending to dig the elf out of her ear with it. Her Papa pulled the hook out of her hand.

"You're the stupid one!" he shouted. "You could burst your eardrum with that hook and make yourself deaf."

"But I must get the elf out!" said she, beginning to cry. Her papa realised that she was not playing tricks. He lifted the sobbing girl up in his arms and carried her into the spare room. Taking a big torch out of a cupboard he shone it in her ear.

"There's no elf in there," he said. "May I drop down dead if I'm telling you a word of a lie. There's only a little bit of wax in there—nothing else!"

Anna stopped sobbing. Her papa carried her to her room. He laid her on the bed, covered her up, planted a

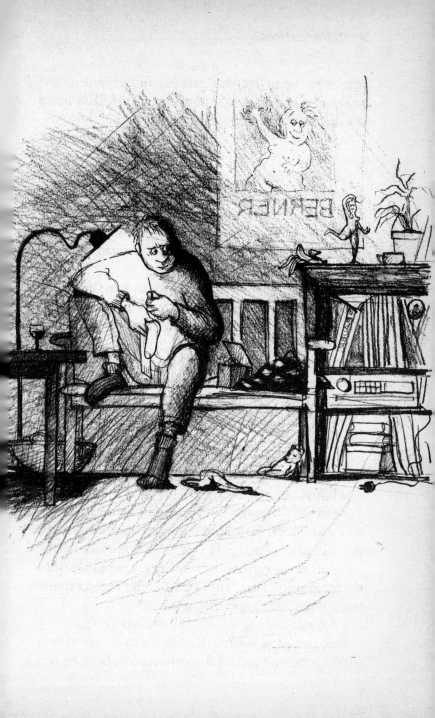

kiss on the tip of her nose, gave her another one on the left cheek, then one on the right cheek and finally kissed her lips. Then he turned out the light and left the room. He left the bedroom door open. That was the way Anna liked it. She never slept well if the door was closed.

She lay in the dark and thought to herself, "The elf probably fell out of my ear when I ran into the living-room; he's probably lying on the floor somewhere. I must look for him. Maybe he has hurt himself..."

Then she fell asleep. So much sobbing had made her very, very tired.

Next morning, well before breakfast, Anna began her search for the elf. She crept on all fours through the flat. She searched in every nook and cranny. But no elf could she find.

Then she saw the vacuum cleaner in Papa's bedroom. So her papa had been hoovering from the crack of dawn! The elf had to be in the cleaner. She opened the lid and took out the bag. It was jam-packed with rubbish. She carried it into the bathroom, put in the stopper in the bath and carefully emptied the rubbish into the bath. There was a lot of nasty stuff in the bath and equally nasty dust hung in the air.

Searching through the yucky garbage Anna found four glass beads, three shirt buttons, two pennies and a pin but before she could complete her search of the contents of the vacuum-cleaner bag her papa came into the room and roared, "I need this like like I need a runny nose. Have you a brain in your head?"

"I'm just looking for the elf," pleaded Anna.

But her papa wasn't listening. Using very strong language he whipped the stopper out of the bath, turned on the hand shower-fitting and tried to wash the nasty stuff down the plug-hole. But all it did was block the waste pipe. Then Papa tore into the kitchen and came back with a packet of caustic pipe cleaner. He threw the whole lot into the pipe. The cleaner hissed and foamed and smelt awful as it disposed of the rubbish.

Anna thought to herself: if the elf did not break his neck when he fell out of my ear or if he did not suffocate with all the dust in the bag or if he did not drown in the water, then certainly the caustic has dissolved him!

She bent over the edge of the bath and whispered into the smelly, hissing, foaming mess, "Rest in peace. Amen!"

Her Papa turned off the shower fitting and rinsed the rest of the caustic away with lots and lots of water. "I swear," he said to Anna, "if anything like this happens again, I'll have you adopted. And that's a promise!"

"Then, at least, I'll get a nice papa," said Anna marching out of the bathroom. As she went she wondered whether she should be glad that the elf was dead or should she be sorry. She decided not to be sorry. The elf hadn't been very nice to her. And he was too small and too whining to be a good playmate. Who needs an elf who was only as big as a little fingernail and had chronic vertigo?

Anyway, Anna did not really want to have anything more to do with elves.

A fortnight later Anna sat at her desk in her room. She was stringing wooden beads in a long chain when someone yawned inside her head—loud and clear and not once but three times! Then the elf spoke: "It seems that I have had a really good sleep."

He belonged to a race of elves that needed a whole lot of sleep. He always slept for up to three weeks at a time,

sometimes up to three months at a time and then he could stay awake for a while—five minutes, half an hour but certainly no longer than an hour. Of course, when he absolutely had to, he could do without sleep for a whole day. But that was totally against his nature.

Anna, quite shocked, thought to herself, damn! the elf isn't dead at all.

Said the elf, "I think it rather mean of you to wish me dead."

Anna thought again, how on earth does the blasted elf know what I'm thinking?

The elf spoke again: "It's obvious: I'm sitting in the very middle of your head. I'm bound to know what your brain is thinking."

Anna would have loved to scream and shake her head like mad. But screaming and head-shaking doesn't help at all against an elf in your skull. She knew that much already. And Papa was not at home. He was at the office.

Only Frau Brauneis was there. She came every weekday morning, cleaned the flat, prepared lunch and minded Anna. Frau Brauneis didn't like to hear children screaming. She was hopping mad if Anna was not a good girl. And as for an elf in the head, you can bet she would understand that even less than Papa.

Anna sat there petrified and white as a sheet. The chain with the coloured wooden beads fell from her hands. The beads slipped from the thread and scattered about the floor. Two of them rolled into the front room just at the very moment when Frau Brauneis walked in there from the living-room. She stepped on one of the beads, went into a slide, bumped into the loo door, crashed to the ground and shrieked something very rude. She pulled out the two beads from under her bottom and began to groan in a dreadful manner. After a time she staggered to her feet and hobbled to Anna's door. Moaning, she held out the two wooden beads.

"You really are an awful child!" she grumbled. "Thanks to you I've severely bruised my coccyx! Looking after you is a dangerous occupation!" Anna didn't answer. She was still white as a sheet and petrified.

"The least you could do is to say you're sorry—" Frau Brauneis kept whittering on "—but it's clear no one has ever taught you manners."

Since Anna didn't answer Frau Brauneis drew herself up and fell to picking up the scattered beads from the floor of the room, all the while grumbling, "A body would need nerves of steel to deal with a child like this. I should get danger money and damages! This has gone too far. I'm going to look for another job."

"The sooner the better!" said the elf in Anna's head. "This old sourpuss needs to go for a complete service and an oil change."

The blood returned to Anna's face and she wasn't petrified any more. The elf, she thought, had some very good ideas.

"Precisely," said the elf.

It wouldn't be half bad, thought Anna, to have the elf to chat to. I'm often quite bored on my own.

"Exactly," said the elf.

But, thought Anna, I can do without him being inside my head. I could build him a nice house—from one of Papa's cigar boxes. Five rooms including kitchen and bathroom should be enough for him.

"Hm-m-m," said the elf. He seemed to be considering the offer.

"I can make him a pretty garden at the front—from green felt. And a fine see-saw from matchsticks.

"Hm-m-m," said the elf. He did not seem to mind the

idea. Anna ran to the stand where on a shelf all her toy cars were displayed. The elf can have his own car, she thought. "Would you like to choose one?" she whispered. "A Mercedes or a BMW? Or would you rather have this Volvo articulated lorry? You could also have this jeep with four-wheel drive. Or would you prefer a railway?"

"You don't have to whisper," said the elf. "You needn't worry. I know everything you think. But now I must regretfully decline your kind offer. It would have been very nice but it wouldn't work. I'm a head-elf. Just as a worm belongs in an apple so I belong in a head. I need the warmth of a head. I can't bear fresh air. A couple of minutes of it and I feel miserable. So it's much better that I stay where I am. But you could get me my cap. I feel quite naked without it!"

Anna wondered where the tiny pointed cap could be. Obviously Frau Brauneis had brushed it out with the rest of the dust.

"The old misery doesn't clean all that thoroughly," said the elf. "Unless I'm mistaken my cap is under your bed beside the upper left-hand leg."

He was right. The cap was under the bed, beside the upper left-hand leg. Anna cleaned the fluff from it. Does it matter, she thought, which ear I stuff it in?

"Generally not," said the elf "but at the moment the right ear suits me better."

So Anna stuffed the violet pointed cap into her right ear. She felt, but only for a short time, a terrible tickle in her ear. Then there was a yawn inside her head. It was loud and clear and repeated twice. Before the elf fell asleep he murmured, "Please don't sneeze. Sneezing will surely waken me up."

Anna was happy, as pleased now to have him as she was frightened before. She thought, it's great to have an elf in the head. Every kid should have one to bring a bit of excitement into her life. This time the elf didn't answer. Anna was sure she could hear him snoring faintly.

2

First Day at School

Anna decided to keep quiet about the elf. It was pretty clear that her Papa still didn't believe in his existence. Besides, the imp hadn't stirred himself for ages. Indeed it was only by the sound of his gentle snoring that Anna knew that he was in her head at all. Perhaps he kept his lively moments for the times when she was fast asleep.

It was on an afternoon in early September that Anna heard the yawning inside her head again. Loud and clear. And three times, one after the other. It was when she was standing in a big store that the elf became active again. She was in the department that sold bags, rucksacks, grips, school satchels and briefcases and was holding a transparent plastic rucksack. Beside her was her mama with a pink schoolbag in her hands. You see, Anna was to go to school for the very first time in two days' time!

"Well, Anna," her mama was saying, "you certainly can't take that see-through thingy. Schoolbags are a bit like rubbish bins and *their* contents should certainly not be visible."

Anna would far rather have had the transparent rucksack as a schoolbag but she nodded and her mama sped to the cash desk. The elf in her head was at that moment far more important than all the satchels in the world! She strolled after her mama and she made herself think, "Good morning, friend elf. It's high time you put in an appearance again."

"I'm sorry but I have no idea about time," said the elf, yawning another little bit. "It gets very confused with me. Sometimes the seconds seem like years, sometimes the years are like seconds."

Anna asked, "How old are you anyway?"

"Again I have no idea," answered the elf. "All I know is, I've been inside an awful lot of heads and I spent a lifetime in most of them!"

Anna's mama paid for the schoolbag, caught hold of Anna's hand and together they left the store. "What shall we do now?" she asked.

"Let's go for a little walk in the wood," suggested Anna. The wood was outside the city. It took a good half-hour to drive there and since her mama would have to be careful of traffic she would not be able to talk much. That would give Anna a chance to chat to the elf.

"The wood?" Mama frowned and looked at her watch. "Anna, I have to be at rehearsal at four," she said. "It's running it a bit close. We'd have time only to go and to come back."

"So how will we pass the time from now till four o'clock?"

"With buns and Coke in the cake-shop."

"Magic!" muttered Anna and off she went to the café with her mama.

As she ate her buns and drank her Coke Anna chatted both to her mama and the elf. That was a bit of a strain but it worked out all right because she didn't actually have to speak to the elf: all she needed to do was to *think*.

From her mama Anna found out that she had to go away in two days' time for a fortnight but she would send Anna a picture postcard with lots of kisses every day.

From the elf she learnt that he had no name and that he was neither male nor female. "We don't have distinctions like that," explained the elf. "We don't have any need for them since we don't get born. We just *are*. So we don't need men and women to bring us into existence."

When Anna told the elf that she would be a schoolgirl in two days, the elf was delighted. "I like school," he said. "And I haven't been there for such a long time. The last head I lived in was already very well educated before I was drawn into it."

The elf did not want to miss that first day at school whatever happened. "Wake me in good time," he said. "Just sneeze three times and I'll be all set."

Then he fell asleep again and Anna was able to devote all her attention to her mother. She told her that Papa had sacked Frau Brauneis. "Now that I am going to school," she said, "we don't need the old sourpuss any more. We'll do the cleaning ourselves and with the money we save we'll be in clover. A month of Brauneis wages could get me a great bike!" Then she asked, "And what am I going to do in the afternoon if you're not there?"

"Liesl is free in the afternoons for the next two weeks," said Mama.

"Definitely not!" cried Anna

"Shall I ask Hannelore?" asked Mama.

"Only if it's absolutely necessary," said Anna. She was disappointed. That her mother of all people had to be away on her first day at school was rotten. Every child is collected by her mama on her first day at school!

"Will you settle for Franz-Josef?" asked Mama. Anna nodded. Franz-Josef was a quite acceptable substitute. "Right," said Mama. "I'll ask him if he has the time. I'll tell you tomorrow what he says." She glanced again at her watch and noticed that it was already ten to four and she was getting uneasy.

"Put me in a taxi," suggested Anna. "If you drive me home yourself you'll not be in time for your rehearsal." Her mama nodded very relieved, paid for the Coke and buns and ran with Anna to the nearest taxi stand. She pressed a kiss on Anna's forehead and a banknote into the taxi-driver's hand and scuttled away.

"Well now," asked the driver, when he stopped in front of Anna's house, "how does it feel to be such a small girl on such a long journey?"

Anna stuck the pink satchel under her arm, said, "I'm a big girl and that was a very short journey!" and climbed out of the taxi. She couldn't bear to be referred to as "little girl." And as for lone taxi-journeys, she was well used to them. At least twice in the week her mama put her into a taxi. But what would that mean to a cabby who was a complete stranger!

The arrangement about Anna and afternoons was simple: Mama was to look after Anna in the afternoon. But Mama could never organise her time properly. Practically every afternoon ended with Mama showing a horrified face and crying, "O God! Now I'm going to be late a*gain*."

Anna was a tremendously parcelled-out child. Afternoons she spent with Mama; evenings, nights and mornings with Papa. Up till now Frau Brauneis was in charge in the forenoon but from the day after tomorrow the forenoon would be schooltime. Mama and Papa took care of her on alternate weekends.

And why? Anna's parents were divorced. Usually the children of divorced parents live with the mother and the father has access once a week for an afternoon; or for a whole fortnight once a year; or once a month; or not at all. It depends on what conditions the divorce judge imposed. The reason for Anna's case being different was Mama's profession. She was an actress but not a famous star whose autograph the public would be anxious to get. She played small parts in a small theatre. But even small theatres have evening performances and occasionally Mama went on tour. Then she travelled for a week or two from town to town and appeared with the company in a different theatre each night. When you have a job like that it's hard to look after a child properly. You can't be at home in the evening and you're still asleep in the morning. And if you have to go on tour it's not very easy to take a child with you.

Anna's papa was always bright as a button in the mornings and loved going to bed early. So it was better for Anna to live with him. The only complication arose when Mama went on tour. Then someone else had to care for Anna in the afternoons for it was not easy for Papa to get time off. He had to be at his desk. On those occasions Liesl, Hannelore or Franz-Joseph took charge. Anna much preferred Franz-Josef as a mother-substitute. He was a young man with no particular job—at different times he was a decorator, a gardener, a chauffeur and a relief postman. Sometimes too he studied a little. Or he minded little children. Anna loved to spend her motherless afternoons with Franz-Josef. But he did not work for nothing; Mama had to pay him. And Mama hadn't much money. Actresses who aren't famous earn very little. Still since it was the start of school Mama treated her daughter to Franz-Josef for the whole two weeks. Anna considered that she was entitled to it. Beginning school is, after all, a pretty important event! At such a time you need someone you love, someone who really listens when you tell about the school, the teacher, the other children, the caretaker, the gym, the school milk and the headmistress. Liesl and Hannelore were useless for that sort of thing. They never listened to Anna. When Anna told them anything they merely nodded their heads and thought of something else. But Franz-Josef was right on. He wanted to know everything about school. Every small detail of what Anna had experienced interested him.

Nevertheless Anna said nothing to him about the elf in her head. The elf did not want that: "Let that be," he warned Anna. "No one can tell how it might turn out. One man, in whose head I used to live, broadcast the fact and everybody took him for a complete idiot. They put him in a hospital with bars on the windows and unbreakable doors. The man was utterly desperate and unhappy and I had to find another head to live in because a miserable and unhappy head makes a very uncomfortable pad."

Anna wanted to avoid such a fate. So she said nothing to Franz-Josef about the elf. But she was absolutely certain that Franz-Josef would have had great fun with the elf. The elf was indeed awake incredibly often since Anna went to school.

On the very first schoolday when Anna had wakened him by sneezing he had managed to stay lively for a whole hour. Anna's school pleased him. "It's a super friendly building," he said praising it. "It's bright and it smells nice. The schools where my previous heads went were pitch-dark and as musty as a zoo cage."

He also approved of Anna's teacher. "Nice woman," he said. "She doesn't shout or make any child stand in the corner and she doesn't raise blisters on people's fingers with her cane."

The elf could scarcely believe it when Anna told him that teachers were not allowed to punish children.

"But I was in a head once," he cried, "that got so many clouts that I almost had the shakes. If your attention drifted for a second from reading, writing and 'rithmetic it was bang, bang, bang on your skull."

That must have been a hundred years ago, thought Anna.

"Could have been," muttered the elf. He had really no idea about time.

Anna was rather surprised that the elf was very uneducated. He knew no more than Anna about writing, no reading and nothing at all about counting. Anna couldn't understand that. She scolded him. "If you have been going to school in so many heads for so many years, then you must have learned something!"

"Of course. That's what I am trying to explain," cried the elf. "I was exactly as clever or as stupid as the head I lived in. Once I was inside the head of a famous mathematics professor. Then I could count better than a computer. And when I was in the head of an interpreter I mastered seven languages—in speech *and* script. But you know, I've hardly left a skull before it has all gone."

When you come to think of it it's really not surprising. An elf who even counting his violet pointy cap isn't any bigger that the littlest fingernail of a six-year-old girl, who has a head as small as a grain of rice! Well, his head must have a brain so tiny that it cannot be seen by the naked eye. What could such a teensy brain, no bigger that a speck of dust, be expected to retain?

Nevertheless, the elf was very useful to Anna at her lessons. True he didn't know any more than she did but he could search through her brain for her to find what she had forgotten. The things people forget lie all over the place in the brain and it's not easy to find them quickly. But the elf could and did, like lightning.

If Anna forgot what homework the teacher had set all she had to do was to ask the elf. He would cry, "Just a second," and root about a little in Anna's head and immediately he'd call, "Here it is. We are to read page ten of the reading book and do a crayon drawing of autumn leaves whirling through the air."

Again when the teacher asked Anna during Counting what twleve take away eight was she did not have to give it much thought. The answer to twelve less eight was already stored in her brain and the elf had it for her at once.

When it came to packing her schoolbag the elf was absolutely super. It simply never happened that he forgot anything. Anna always came to school with everything she needed. And if the elf was too tired in the evening to tell Anna what should go into the pink satchel he reminded her about it at breakfast. It suited Anna down to the ground but for the elf it was a wearisome life. He wasn't getting his usual amount of sleep. He yawned all the time—not just when he woke or before he went to sleep. And Anna had to yawn at the same time for yawning is very catching. Another thing was that the elf's voice had become quite hoarse. He wasn't used to so much talking.

3

Christmas—and Grandparents!

On the last schoolday before Christmas, after the Christmas party, after the teacher had wished all the children "A merry Christmas and a happy New Year," said the elf to Anna, "Well, that's the last straw! I intend to sleep throughout the whole period of the Christmas festivities. I'm absolutely shattered. Don't sneeze me awake; otherwise I'll have a total physical breakdown!"

But Christmas is coming, thought Anna to him. With a tree and presents! You can't sleep it all away. Christmas is the most super time of year!

"Not for me," muttered the elf, yawning and snoring loudly at the same time.

And I wanted to make him his own little Christmas tree from seven pine needles, thought Anna, and to make him a present of a new pointy hat, made out of crimson silk.

Anna considered sneezing the elf awake so that she might explain to him how wonderful Christmas was but she decided to let things be. She wouldn't risk his having a total physical breakdown—whatever that might be. I'll let the fellow sleep now and not sneeze him awake till the time of opening the gifts.

On Christmas Eve Anna spent the whole morning stuck in her room trying to stick together seven pine needles to make a Christmas tree and to sew a silk cap with a little woollen bobble. But she didn't manage it. So she decided to let the elf sleep through Christmas. Since she had no gift for him she mustn't risk his having a total physical collapse.

Anna had explained to the elf that Christmas was "the most super time of year" but she did not really believe it herself. She said it only because all the other children said it and she did not want to be the odd one out. In fact Anna dreaded Christmas a bit because for her it was a rather complicated holiday—on account of her separated parents!

Anna's papa and mama were not such deadly enemies that they could not agree to spend Christmas together for her sake. But a lovely, long, father-mother-child

Christmas Eve could nevertheless not be arranged because Mama's parents travelled from Linz for Christmas and Papa's from Graz. And Mama's parents did not want to meet Papa's parents; and Papa's parents wanted to have nothing to do with Mama's parents. Mama's parents said that Papa was responsible for the split and Papa's parents said that Mama was to blame. If the two sets of parents met they started an argument about it. And Christmas is, after all, the festival of peace. One can do without bickering at such a time.

So this is the way Anna had to celebrate Christmas: early in the afternoon of Christmas Eve she had Christmas with her Papa and Mama in Papa's flat. Then Papa drove to the station to fetch his parents while she went with Mama to *her* flat. There she had Christmas with her mama and Mama's parents. Then Anna's father came and took her to have Christmas with his parents in his

flat. On the morning of Christmas Day Mama collected her again. On St Stephen's Day she was back with her father. On Christmas Day she had to endure her mama's parents, the next day her papa's.

Anna did not fancy her grandparents much. One lot did not like her mama, the other lot took a dim view of her father. And both lots were to blame for Anna not having a lovely long Christmas time with her parents. They could give much better gifts, thought Anna peevishly, darn them, if they just sent the things by post. This year the short father-mother-child party in Papa's flat wasn't even nice. Papa went off in the morning to buy a fir-tree. At midday he came back with a giant that stretched from floor to ceiling. "I must have been a bit out in my measurements," he sighed. The trunk of the gigantic tree was so thick that all of the Christmas-tree holders that Papa brought up from the cellar were too small. So Papa nailed together a cross of planks and sawed a large hole in the centre of the cross for the trunk. It took quite a while. When Mama came Papa had just fixed the tree upright in its cross and so it was completely bare. Anna, Mama and Papa worked like crazy to decorate the tree with candles, baubles, threaded sweets and tinsel. And every few minutes Mama would say, "Now that should be enough." But it was far from enough. Mama kept saying it as it got later and later. On the dot of six her parents would be outside the door ringing the bell and cheesed off if nobody was there to open it.

Papa declared that the tree looked absolutely marvellous but he was fibbing because he had to be at the station exactly at six.

Anna complained. The pink meringues, the chocolate

gingerbread, the gold stars, the little tin Santa Clauses, and coloured paper-chains which Anna had made with her own hands—they had to be on the tree too. And the silver medallions and gold pine-cones.

Papa and Mama could see her point and they continued with the decoration of the tree. But it's not much crack to dress a Christmas tree with two people who keep looking at the clock and can't hide their nervousness.

At last about half past five Anna was reasonably content with the look of the tree. That left only just twenty minutes for the Christmas celebrations. Anna did not have time to have a look at all the presents that Papa and Mama had left for her under the tree.

"We've got to scram, Anna," said Mama. "You'll be coming back here tonight anyway!"

Papa consoled Anna. "You'll still have a few surprises waiting for you later."

Anna puffed after her mother as they rushed to the car. The street glittered with frost. "That's all we need," moaned Mama. "I really hate ice on the roads. It means that I'll have to crawl. And the wrinklies will be waiting at the door. And that'll mean another three-act drama."

The parents were not standing at the apartment door when Anna and her mother came charging up the stairs. But Mama was hardly inside the porch when the phone rang. It was Mama's mother and she announced that she was still in St Pölten—because of the black ice. "Your father cannot drive at more than twenty kilometres an hour. It'll be at least two hours before we get there."

"How stupid," blazed Anna. "The three of could have had our Christmas in peace, but *you* had to run."

"How was I to know that there'd be ice on the motorway! Because of all that decorating of the tree I never realised that the streets were icing up. As well as that the ice didn't keep the train late. And I can very well do without seeing my ex-in-laws again."

"And what I want doesn't matter to you!" said Anna.

"That's not true!" cried Mama."Don't reproach me at Christmas above all times that we are not a normal family. Apart from the matter of divorced parents it is perfectly normal. Every third child is in a similar situation."

"Every second child has a dog—and I've none!" said Anna.

"I'd have bought you one already but your father is against it. He will not allow a dog into his flat—he's adamant."

Anna was grumpy: "I never said that you should give me a dog."

"Oh, yes you did!" cried Mama.

"No I didn't!" cried Anna. "All I said was that if to have divorced parents is normal, because that is the way with every third child, then it is also normal that I should have a dog, because that is the way with every *second* child. Why have I the nasty normal things and not the normal nice things? That's what I meant about the dog."

"Och, Anna!" murmured Mama putting on her sad sausage-dog face. When her mother looked so sad Anna could never stay cross with her.

"It's all right," said Anna. "Let's switch on the Christmas tree."

The tree in Mama's apartment wasn't very tall—about

the same height as Anna. Its only decorations were white candles, white angel's hair and white baubles.

"Shouldn't we wait till the grandparents come?" said Mama. "You know what your granny's like. She'll feel very affronted if she sees that the candles are already lit."

"Okay, we'll wait so," said Anna, turning up the television.

When Mama's parents finally arrived, they first of all went into great detail about the black ice on the motorway and of a pile-up which thankfully they just avoided. Then Grandmother had to go to the bathroom to "freshen-up" and get changed into the party clothes she had brought in her case. "In the car," she said to Anna, "I would have 'seated' the pleats in my good skirt."

Granny stayed ages in the bathroom. Three times Mama knocked on the bathroom door and called out, "Mammy, hurry and finish. We have to give out the Christmas presents before it's too late."

It was almost nine o'clock when Granny with freshly curled hair, powdered cheeks, a three-strand pearl necklace round her neck and a gold belt about her middle, stalked out of the bathroom.

Mama rang a little bell, Grandpa lit the candles on the tree and the doorbell tinkled. It was Papa!

"Why is *he* here?" asked Granny looking indignant.

"Because it's on the dot of nine," said Anna. She would love to have ripped out her Granny's tongue. As Mama went to open the door of the flat Granny called after her, "Tell him we've only arrived. Let him come back in an hour's time."

Grandpa said to Anna, "Now you can look at what we've brought you in peace. You'll have plenty of time."

Mama came back into the room.

"Has he gone?" asked Granny.

"He's waiting in the kitchen," answered Mama. She didn't look very happy. Anna realised that she she could not possibly look at her presents while her Papa skulked in the kitchen. As well, the kitchen wasn't all that tidy. Mama had cooked the Christmas dinner there, and when Mama cooked she left behind a lot of dirty dishes—which had not yet been washed up. Anna spoke: "I prefer to look at my presents tomorrow!"

"Child!" shrieked Granny.

"Let it be," said Grandpa to Granny. Anna decided to leave the room and had got as far as the door when Granny called, "Do I not even get a goodbye kiss?" Anna would gladly have said "no" but she well knew that Granny would complain to her Mama and reproach her that she was not bringing Anna up properly.

So Anna went like a good little girl and gave her Granny a smacking kiss on the powdered cheeks—and gave Grandpa one on his sideburns. The Grandpa-kiss seemed to her less unpleasant. Then she ran into the hallway and put on her coat. "I'm ready, Papa," she called into the kitchen. Papa came out. He had his fur cap already on his head. "Let's go." He did not look all that happy. Mama stood at the living-room door and whispered, "How nasty! You've hurt me deeply, Anna."

"Till tomorrow then," said Anna and tried to smile.

Anna's third Christmas celebration was a success only at the start. She was in no hurry now and had plenty of peace to open her presents. And she was delighted about that. She had got plenty: a wristwatch with a Mickey Mouse on the dial, a lot of games, roller-skates, a doll's

house with an upstairs and an attic, books, a Garfield to put on her necklace, a white ski-suit, a mini-supermarket with lots of shelves, filled with tiny packets of washing powder and noodles. There were also three little trolleys. And at the check-out sat a little cashier made out of modelling-clay. You could bend the arms and legs into any position you liked.

The other Grandpa and Granny had brought as a present a giant package. That package was as big as a cupboard, and so heavy that Anna could not budge it. "That travelled by the express," said Grandpa proudly. "We couldn't get it into the compartment!"

"And I had to buy a roof-rack for the car to get the thing home from the station," said Papa.

In the big-as-a-wardrobe box was a completely crazy present: a climbing-tower with a slide and a foam-rubber mat which was to be placed under the tower. So if you fell off the climber or came too quickly down the slide you wouldn't hurt yourself. Grandpa and Papa worked till midnight to assemble the tower. They set it up in the living-room. Anna's room was too small for the huge frame.

Anna was charmed with her present. So pleased was she that had almost decided that this Christmas Eve was one of the great ones. Then almost at the end things got rotten again. Here is what happened: Anna was lying in bed; she had her Mickey Mouse watch on her wrist, the Garfield on her necklace and she was leafing through one of the books she had got. It occurred to her that she could do a little climbing and a little sliding—even though it was so late! The grandparents and Papa were sitting in Papa's study. When Anna sneaked quietly into the living-room the three must not have noticed. They would have been absolutely opposed to Anna's moving about after midnight. So Anna slipped quietly into the living-room—to the climbing tower. The door to Papa's study was open just a crack. And Anna heard Papa say, "Really, sometimes it's all a bit much!"

Anna wanted to know what Papa found sometimes all a bit too much and crept to the door of the den.

"It's clear that a man cannot manage," said Granny.

"It's no better for a divorced woman with a child," said Papa. "On the contrary, most of them don't have a husband who takes over the child every afternoon."

"That may be so," said Granny. "But it's not much of a life for you. Besides, it's not necessary. After all you have a mother who is still sprightly and has loads of time."

Bloody hell, thought Anna, Granny will wreck us altogether. But it was getting even worse! Granny said, "We have a big house and a huge garden, the ideal environment for a child. And sure you can come every weekend for a visit. We'd love to see you, even oftener."

Anna threw the door open. "Never, never, never, never in my whole life," she screamed and began to sob. Papa jumped up. "Really, Anna, if you had waited a second longer you'd have heard that I am in total agreement with your 'never, never, never, never in my whole life.'" He tossed her high and laughed. "What would I do without you?" he demanded as he bit Anna in the neck, but only as a joke and very gently.

"But what about the times when I get too much for you?" Anna was not yet pacified.

"It's not you at all!" said Papa. "It's mostly the

cleaning and the cooking. But we can always get another sourpuss if I can't manage any more. We'll live almost like lords." That eased Anna. Papa carried her into her room. "Let the woman talk," he said quietly. "She doesn't mean wicked by it."

"It *was* very wicked, all the same," said Anna.

Papa gave Anna a kiss on the tip of her nose, one on the right cheek, one on the left and one on the mouth. "Anna, I'd be lost without you in my life," he said as he left the room.

Anna sat up again, took a paper hankie out of the drawer of her bedside table and blew her nose. Because of her sobbing her nose was full of mucus.

Stupid Granny, she thought, talking utter rubbish. Had to spoil Christmas on me! Still things didn't go as *she* wanted. Never, never, never, never in her whole life!

Anna was no longer afraid that she would be taken away by Papa's parents but she was no longer quite as happy as she should have been. She thought, just as well that I didn't sneeze the elf awake. It wasn't exactly a showpiece Christmas celebration!

4

A Real Creep

When the holidays came to an end, the elf was still asleep. Anna sneezed him awake on the morning of the first day back at school but the elf merely said, "I don't feel so great," and fell asleep again.

Anna gave him another fortnight's grace, then sneezed him awake again. The elf yawned, not three times after each other but rather thirty times in succession.

"Anything special?" he asked.

Nothing special, thought Anna. Everything's dead boring!

"Then I'll have another bit of shuteye," said the elf and snored away like good-o.

Anna was disappointed. She had roused the elf because there was nothing happening, because she was bored, because she wanted a bit of chat with him. The teacher practised with the "weaker children," particularly oral reading. Anna could read very well. Both quietly and aloud! It wasn't therefore very likely that she would be called by the teacher to do oral reading. Because of sheer disappointment with the sleep-obsessed elf Anna said aloud, "You dumb elf!"

Immediately Hermann, who sat beside her, punched her in the ribs and hissed, "You dumb elf, yourself!" He thought that when she said "Dumb elf!" she meant him.

Hermann was generally a problem! Anna had made a really heavy mistake about him. On the first day at school she had very much liked the look of him. He was unusually good-looking. He had long dark curls. And big blue eyes. And a tiny, absolutely straight nose with three darling freckles on its tip. He also had blindingly white, perfect teeth. And his clothes were the trendiest.

When Hermann asked Anna on the first day if she would sit beside him, she had nodded happily and thought that she had hit the jackpot. The elf hadn't taken to Hermann. "Well now, I don't know," he said. "I have no respect for that type. I don't like that guy at all!"

You don't know him at all, thought Anna to him.

"I have my suspicions," the elf had said.

Those are not suspicions, Anna had thought, they are prejudgements. And you shouldn't do that sort of thing.

At that the elf got very offended. "Okay," he muttered, "I won't say another word against that flash guy. But you'll have your eyes opened for you yet. You will see that I am right."

And the elf was right. Hermann was a real creep. He was mean. He never stopped showing off. And he continually complained to the teacher about Anna. When Anna's red crayon had crumbled and she wanted to borrow a red crayon from Hermann, only for two little lines, he held on to his crayon box as if his life depended upon it, and whined, "Why should I let you use my crayons? Look after your own things better and then they won't break."

When any of Anna's exercise books were even a little bit over on Hermann's half of the desk, he would put up his right hand, wave it about in the air, "Please, miss, Anna is taking up all the room."

And when once Anna felt very hungry during a lesson and secretly under the desk took a bite of her snack—although it was forbidden to eat during class—Hermann's waving arm was seen again and he sneaked to the teacher, "Please, miss, Anna is eating and she is spilling crumbs all over my trousers."

And Hermann's boasting was really gross. A child would say, "We have a house with five rooms," and Hermann would boast, "Well, we have a house with ten rooms!" Everybody knew that Hermann hadn't a house at all but lived in a flat above a supermarket. Another child would say, "My car racetrack is seven metres long," and Hermann would say, "My track is seventy metres long!" And every child knew that there was no track that was that long. A child would say, "We have a dog, a long-haired dachshund," and Hermann would say, "But we have three dogs, St Bernards, with much longer hair." All the children knew that he hadn't a dog at all.

That was Hermann and none of the kids could stick him. They all said to Anna, "Anna, you are really very unlucky to have to sit beside that twit."

Anna thought she was very unlucky as well. Especially since she knew exactly whom she would like to sit beside. She wanted to be beside Peter. Once she got to know the other children well she realised that. She really fancied Peter. He wasn't as good-looking as Hermann and his clothes were not as fashionable. He had really short fair hair, grey eyes, a little snub nose, and his teeth were crooked. Between his two upper front teeth was a broad gap through which he could whistle—nearly as loud as if he had a referee's whistle in his mouth. Peter's trousers were threadbare and patched because he had inherited them from his big brother. His T-shirts were always stained because he loved to roll about in the dirt of the school yard during break.

Anna was always to be found with Peter during break, and after school when Anna stood at the corner waiting for Mama he stood with her until Mama's car came along the street.

Often Peter would say to Anna, "It was really dumb that we didn't get sitting beside each other on the first day at school." The boy next to Peter was called Michi. Anna once asked him if he would change places with her. But Michi refused. "If you sat beside Susi," said he, "I'd change places with you immediately!"—Michi fancied Susi a little—"but to sit beside that Hermann? Not on your life. There'd be murder done! I'd finish that fink off!"

Anna confided in Papa how miserable she was on account of Hermann. Papa said that she should simply ignore the "creep" and put up with things cheerfully. He suggested, "Have a good laugh when he tries to get funny with you."

But that wasn't very good advice. When Anna laughed at Hermann he got furious and punched her in the stomach or the ribs, pinched her arm or stamped on her toes, pulled her hair or spat at her. And since Anna did not want to make a "grass" of herself like Hermann, she couldn't complain to the teacher about the bullying. She could not properly defend herself either because she had no practice in boxing, pinching, hair-pulling, stamping or spitting. Again and again when Hermann was really revolting Anna tried to defend herself but her kicking and punching proved miserably inadequate. And she couldn't bring herself to spit: that would be too creepy altogether.

Anna also confided in Mama about her trouble. Mama wanted to go to the school to see the teacher: "I will insist that you be separated from that horror. The teacher cannot expect you to share a desk with that!"

Anna was dead against that. She explained to Mama, "There's not another empty place in the classroom. If I got away from Hermann some other kid would have to take my place. That I wouldn't do to anyone. No way!"

"Dear me," said Mama, "If you're so noble, child, then no one can help you!"

"Maybe there is…" retorted Anna

"And who is it that can help you?" asked Mama. But that Anna did not tell her mother. Anna had hopes of the elf. She thought, when that oversleeping fellow has a wakeful period again I'll discuss it with him. The elf is a smart cookie; he'll know what to do to settle that Hermann.

The elf decided in the middle of February at last to wake up properly. "Now I'm fighting fit," he promised Anna. "From now on I can manage any number of lively mornings!" Then he asked: "Where are we anyway?"

We're in Mama's flat, thought Anna.

"Is that the woman who insisted that you take the pink satchel although you preferred the transparent rucksack?" asked the elf. Anna nodded. At that Liesl came into the room. Liesl sublet part of Mama's apartment. It was an expensive apartment and Mama needed someone to help with the rent.

"Your mama looks a lot prettier today," said the elf.

"Not true at all!" cried Anna aloud. She was indignant that the elf thought Liesl prettier than Mama.

"What's not true at all?" asked Liesl.

"Pardon?" said Anna in amazement.

Liesl said, "You shouted just now 'not true at all.' So I'm asking you what's not true at all!"

"I, I didn't say a word!"

"Funny kid," murmured Liesl and left the room.

"Stupid cow," said Anna under her breath.

"Don't you like your mama?"asked the elf.

It would be a lot better if stupid Liesl were my mama, thought Anna.

"Ah!" cried the elf, "if that's not your mama it's no surprise that she's much prettier today."

My mama is prettier than Liesl, thought Anna.

"Definitely not," said the elf.

Absolutely, thought Anna.

"Don't fight with me about it," said the elf. "We don't always have to have the same views." Then he giggled and said, "When I look around me inside your brain, I see that we are in agreement about another business. I'm glad of that. I like to be in the right."

I haven't a clue what you're talking about, thought Anna.

"I am referring to the one who shares your desk,"giggled the elf. "It's something that we cannot overlook. Your head is full of Herr Mann! [That's how the elf pronounced Hermann.] And I gather from that you are full of anger and rage at this Herr Mann!"

Anna thought, it's not something to smirk about.

"Forgive me," said the elf. Now his voice sounded serious again. If things are so bad we must do something about it. For my sake! I do not want to live with rage and anger."

Then set your mind to it, thought Anna. In the meantime I'll do my homework, which is really a lot today. And I am of no use to you at all in your thinking. I have been pondering the matter for weeks and I've not come up with anything useful.

When Anna was finished with her homework she asked the elf if he had devised anything to use against Hermann.

"Not completely," murmured the elf, "but I'm absolutely bristling with ideas and soon I'll have a brainwave."

Then I won't disturb you, thought Anna. She took her homework copy and went to see her mama. She was in Liesl's room, discussing the telephone bill with her.

"If you ring Italy three times in the week you'll have to pay more than half the amount!"

"If it comes to that," said Liesl, "you blather for three hours a day with your darling Oskar and it works out the same."

"Me? Three hours a day?" squealed Mama. "I hardly use the phone for ten minutes in the day. Oskar rings me and it costs us nothing!"

"Don't make me laugh!" shouted Liesl and laughed evilly.

"At the moment you certainly earn more than I do," shouted Mama, "so don't be so miserly. Pay two-thirds of the bill and we'll say no more about it."

"If you didn't continually buy trendy gear," screamed Liesl, "you could manage on the money you have."

Before Mama could answer, Anna said, "I have my arithmetic homework finished. Will you check it for me, Mama?"

"Your homework will have to wait!" growled Liesl to Anna. "Do you not realise that I have something important to discuss with your mama?"

Anna stuck her tongue out at Liesl. "You are being mean to Mama. She's not always buying gear. And you ride in her car all over the place and use her petrol and you never fill the tank!"

Liesl closed her eyes and sighed deeply, as if to say, God in heaven, why do you plague me every afternoon with this horrible kid?

"Anna, mind your own business," said Mama. She was clearly displeased that Anna had brought up the matter of the petrol.

"It's true!" cried Anna. "Yesterday we were down to the last drop of petrol when we got to the filling-station."

Liesl hissed at Mama, "Nice of you to talk about me behind my back!"

Mama did not answer. She lifted Anna's exercise. She had done twenty-four sums and Mama could find only one mistake.

"Very good, Anna," said Mama, gave Anna back her copy and started fighting with Liesl again, this time not about the phone bill but about the petrol.

Anna went back into Mama's living-room and corrected the mistake. It was quite simple: all she had to do was to change a three to a nine.

Well, she asked the elf, has the brainwave occurred?

"In a way," said the elf, a little bit hesitantly.

Tell me, demanded Anna impatiently.

"I must still ponder the matter," said the elf. "It could be quite dangerous for me because the open air is harmful for me and because I'm no hero!"

Why a hero? What is your plan? Anna squirmed with impatience.

"Okay," sighed the elf. "Tomorrow at the school I will be inserted into the head of Herr Mann and look around to try to discover why the boy is so nasty. When we know that we can more easily discover the remedy."

You are a genius, thought Anna.

"Thanks," said the elf. Then he spoke further: "No tricks, please. I don't want you to prevent my getting back in here. I like living with you."

Would I do the like of that? Anna shook her head. You're the best friend that I have.

"Really?" asked the elf. He snuffled a little. Apparently he was moved to tears.

5

The Elf Makes a Decision

Next day before the eight o'clock bell, when the children were still standing about the classroom and the teacher was gossiping with the teacher of the class next door, the elf spoke. "As far as I'm concerned I'm ready."

"Me too," whispered Anna. She was tremendously excited.

"Right, let's do it then," sighed the elf. "But exactly as we planned it. Otherwise things will go skew-whiff. And you know well that fresh air doesn't suit me."

Okay, exactly according to plan, thought Anna. The plan was as follows: Anna was to wait until Hermann was sitting in his place. Then she had to get really close to Hermann, until their shoulders were actually touching. And she had to stay like that until the elf could get out of her ear onto her neck, clamber along her shoulder and get onto Hermann's shoulder. After that it was up to the elf! Just at the next bell Anna had to be on the ball again. Then she had to push her shoulder against Hermann's so that the elf could find his way home.

For this undertaking Anna had also changed her hairstyle. Her hair which usually was gathered into a ponytail at the back of her head today hung about her ears and lay in pretty curls on her shoulders. The elf had cover as long as he was climbing about Anna. And since Hermann had black ringlets which covered his ears, the only part of the elf's route which was actually dangerous was the part over Hermann's shoulder and neck. Only there would he be visible!

Anna sat down on her chair and waited. Hermann went from the wastepaper basket, where he had sharpened two coloured pencils, to his desk. He sat down beside Anna. At that instant the school bell began to buzz. The teacher came into the room and went to her table. The children who were still standing about ran to their places. Anna thought go! and leant her shoulder against Hermann's. Her fear that he would pull away from her proved groundless. Hermann pressed his shoulder against hers, pushed himself right up against her and hissed at her: "Stop shoving. You're over in my half! Get back to

your own half again!" Anna did not give way! She pushed herself hard against Hermann and squinted at his neck with her heart in her mouth. The elf was creeping up Hermann's red polo-neck. Without his pointy hat! He disappeared immediately into Hermann's black curls.

Anna relaxed the pressure on Hermann's shoulder and sat correctly again in her own half. She ran her fingers through her curls. Yes! there was the tiny pointy hat. She took it out of her hair and put it in her trousers pocket. And stared straight ahead. Right at the teacher. The teacher opened up the blackboards, took a piece of white chalk and looked round the class. "Which of you would like to draw snowflakes?" A couple of kids put up their hands. Hermann didn't raise his. He dunted Anna in the ribs with his elbow, clearly as a punishment for "shoving."

The teacher saw what he did and said, "I think that

Hermann is the best one to draw snowflakes. Maybe that will bring him to his senses."

Hermann rose and pointed to Anna. "She pushed first," he cried.

"Hermann," said the teacher, "don't whine at every little thing. Come out immediately and make nice snowflakes."

Hermann went to the board and the teacher placed the chalk in his hand. He was about to do the drawing when he suddenly made a face, jerked his mouth open and let the chalk fall.

"Hermann, what's the matter?" asked the teacher.

"Excuse me, something is hurting my head!" moaned Hermann. He bent to get the chalk but he did not straighten. He stayed there bent double and pressed both his hands against his ears. "It stings," he shouted. "It stings awfully."

The teacher picked up the chalk and gazed in astonishment at Hermann.

"Right, Hermann, go back to your place at once," she said. "Gerti will do the snowflakes!"

Gerti skipped up to the board while Hermann went, still bent and with his hands over his ears, back to his place. He sat down on his chair and began to moan. He did not move his hands from his ears.

"Now, Hermann, what on earth are we to do with you?" asked the teacher.

She seemed completely nonplussed.

"He is really a sniveller," said Gerti to the teacher. The teacher didn't nod in agreement but she seemed to be of the same opinion. She went to Hermann's desk, felt his forehead and said, "You have no temperature, Hermann."

Hermann pressed his hands harder against his ears and waggled his head. "I can't bear it, " he whined. "Stop it. Now!"

That was something Anna hadn't reckoned on—that an elf in the head should cause pain. It had tickled a bit, all right, when the elf climbed in. Either Hermann was particularly sensitive to pain or else things were altogether different in his head than in Anna's.

All the kids in the classroom stared at the whining, shivering Hermann. The teacher said to Anna, "Be a dear and take Hermann to the headmistress. She'll phone home about him and get someone to fetch him."

Anna stood up. Her knees were shaking as if they were made of jelly. What was going to happen now? It was awful—it was terrible.

Hermann hadn't heard what the teacher had said. He had kept his hands tight against his ears. Anna pulled a hand from the ear by which the elf had got in. It took all her strength. "Come along!" she cried.

Hermann stood up. Anna held on to the hand so that he could not place it over his ear again. She wanted to give the elf a chance to escape. She led Hermann out of the classroom along the corridor up to the office. "Come *on,*" she pleaded. She was speaking to the elf but Hermann thought that it was to him and he moaned, "It's so jaggy. I can't go any faster.

The door of the office was open. The headmistress sat behind her desk. She looked up as Anna arrived with Hermann.

"What's this, children?" she asked

"I have an awful jaggy pain in my head," screamed Hermann, ripped his hand out of Anna's and covered his ears with both hands again.

"Clearly a middle-ear infection," said the head, looking worried.

Anna thought, I must definitely stick close to Hermann in case I lose my elf. The head pushed Hermann towards a chair. "Sit there, you poor fellow," she said. Hermann flopped on the seat. The head went to the phone. "What's his name?" she asked Anna.

"Hermann Schnack, 1B!" said Anna.

The head leafed through the book that held the addresses and numbers of all the pupils. "We have it here—Schnack," and dialled. Anna bent down close to Hermann. She acted as if she were full of sympathy for him. "Hang in there; don't be afraid. Somehow you'll get back!"

The head was touched as she gazed from the telephone to Anna. She had no idea that Anna was not talking to Hermann but to the elf. "You're a good comforter. Stay with him until his mama comes." Then she screwed a sheet of paper into her typewriter and typed a letter.

Anna tried inconspicuously to pull Hermann's paws from his head but she failed. Hermann stolidly kept both hands over his ears. However his fingers were not tightly pressed together. Maybe, thought Anna, the elf has already slipped through Hermann's fingers. Perhaps he is even now sitting somewhere in Hermann's curls and is scared stiff because of his vertigo. Anna stroked Hermann's head gently but she found no trace of the elf.

Things happened quickly then. Hermann's mother stalked through the door, said to the headmistress, "Thank you for the phone call," rushed up to Hermann, cried, "My poor baby," gathered Hermann into her arms, said to the headmistress, "My baby must go straight to bed," and scuttled off with her giant baby in her arms.

"Now, go back to class," said the head to Anna, "and don't be worried about your friend. He must be unusually susceptible to pain." Anna nodded and stumbled out of the office. She stopped at one of the corridor windows from which you could view the street.

In front of the school gate a taxi was parked. Hermann's mother came out of the school and ran across to it. The driver got out of the car, pulled the rear door open, Hermann's mother with her big baby climbed inside, the driver slammed the door shut and climbed into the taxi by the driver's door. Then it sped off.

Anna went back to class. She was awfully sad. She sat in her place and tried to pay attention to the teacher but she did not follow a single word that the teacher said. She did not even notice that the board was covered with snowflakes. All she had in her head was, my elf, my poor elf! Even during break Anna sat in her seat. Peter came to see her and offered her a bite of his apple. Anna shook her head.

"Not hungry?" asked Peter

Anna shook her head.

"Are you cross with me?"

Anna shook her head.

"Hey you!" Peter chucked her on the nose. "What's up?"

"Nothing." What should she say to Peter? Maybe: my elf in the head had a look around Hermann's brain, and now I don't know whether he is still inside Hermann's skull or lying somewhere helpless. Maybe someone has already trampled him to death!

Obviously Anna couldn't say that to Peter. He would think she was bonkers!

"My throat's sore," she croaked. She thought that might be a convincing excuse.

Peter put his arm about her shoulder. "I'll bet it was that creep Hermann who smit you," he said. "You should be in bed. I'll tell the teacher."

Anna wasn't as quick to respond as she usually was without her elf in the head but she twigged immediately: this is great; this is a golden opportunity!

Peter took his arm from about Anna's shoulder and ran to see the teacher.

A few minutes later Anna was sitting in the office and the headmistress was phoning again. First she called Mama's place. Anna could have told her that no one would lift the receiver. Liesl was on early shift today. She was a waitress in an espresso bar. And Mama was broadcasting. Yesterday she had told Anna that she had to go to the studio "at an unearthly hour." She was rehearsing a radio play.

Then the head rang Papa's office to learn that Anna's papa was "on his way" and would arrive just at noon.

"Well, Anna, what shall we do with you?" asked the head.

Anna dug down into the front of her pullover and drew out her key-chain. Anna always carried the keys to both her father's and her mother's flats on a gold chain which hung about her neck.

"Papa's flat is just round the corner," croaked Anna. "And my feet are just fine. And because of my throat I won't run." That convinced the head. She went with Anna to the cloakroom, wound her scarf three times round her neck, told her to go straight home to bed and brought her as far as the school gate. Anna croaked, "Thank you, miss," and off she went taking short, rather weary steps. She moved exactly the way a child sick with a sore throat would.

6

Being Nice to Hermann

Straight to the corner of the street marched Anna in the direction of her papa's flat. Then she peeked back at the school. The headmistress had gone from the school gate. Anna breathed a sigh of relief, then turned around and ran down the street past the school, turned two corners heading for the supermarket. Hermann lived in the supermarket building.

Anna entered the building and climbed four flights of twenty steps until she was outside a door with the nameplate *Schnack* on it. She pressed the bell beside the plate and Hermann's mother opened the door of the apartment. Astounded, she looked down at Anna. "Aren't you the little girl who was in the administration office with my baby?" she asked.

Anna nodded. "Yes," she said. "I'm Anna and I'd like to see Hermann."

"How is it that school is over for the day?" asked Hermann's mother.

"If you please, I don't know," lied Anna and she must have seemed very stupid because when class finishes at half past nine the schoolchildren know well the reason for such an unexpected bit of luck. However Hermann's

mother asked no more questions and led Anna into the nursery to Hermann.

He was lying in his bed in sky-blue sheets and turning the pages of a Mickey Mouse comic.

"Our dotey is much better now," said the mother. "His head doesn't hurt him any more."

God in heaven, thought Anna, that is mega-terrible. Does it mean that my elf is no longer in his skull?

"But in one of my ears there's still a stupid tickle."

Thank God, thought Anna, then everything is creamy! Who but the elf would be scratching about in Hermann's ear? She went to Hermann's bed and sat on the edge.

"Now, do you see, precious," said the mother. "You always claim that none of the children can stick you. Yet here is Anna come to visit you. She wouldn't do that if she weren't very fond of you." Hermann's mother beamed, apparently in extreme happiness.

"Indeed, yes, I'm fond of him," said Anna, feeling very, very mendacious.

Hermann looked at Anna in astonishment. He was about to speak when the mother cried, "Anna, you must be hungry! Would you like a slice of cake or would you prefer a piece of nut strudel?"

"Don't give her any nut strudel," grumbled Hermann. "That's what I want."

"But precious, Anna is your guest," said the mother. "One's guest must get the same things that one likes oneself."

"I would much rather have the cake," said Anna.

Hermann's mother went to fetch the cake. When she left the room Anna bent over Hermann's right ear. "Where does it tickle?" she asked and stared into the ear.

"At first it tickled deep inside," wailed Hermann, "but now all of a sudden it is more to the outside."

Anna held her breath. There on the outside of Hermann's right ear the elf's head appeared.

"Now the tickling is practically gone," Hermann told her with relief.

"That's really great," whispered Anna. She placed her hand under Hermann's right ear. The elf crept out of the auditory canal into the outer ear, slid over the lobe and jumped into the palm of Anna's hand. Anna pulled her hand away from Hermann's ear.

"I am absolutely delighted," she said.

"Me too," said Hermann.

Anna lifted her hand carefully to her own ear and inclined her head so that the elf could comfortably climb in. And she handed him the pointy hat which he had lost in the previous entry.

Welcome home, my darling elf, she thought. How are you? I have had terrible worries about you.

At first the elf did not speak. He just sobbed heart-rendingly. Then he murmured, "I'll tell you something: the inside of that guy's head is really something. There's nothing there but sheer lunacy. Brrrrrr! A prison would be heaven compared with a spell in that skull!"

At that the elf yawned once and was dead asleep before he could yawn for a second time.

Anna wanted very much to get up at once and go straight home. But she did not wish to be impolite. She was also munching gamely a piece of the hideously sweet and hideously fatty cake that Hermann's mother had brought. And because Hermann wanted it she was playing Old Maid with him. After the third hand it got to her.

Hermann was behaving abominably. Because he *had* to win he held his cards very tight—when he had only two cards left in his hand and neither was the Old Maid—and squawked when Anna wanted to take those cards, "No-no-no, I won't let them go."

"That's because he is very sick," explained the mother. "When one is sick one gets a little odd."

"He's just the same when he's well," said Anna and stood up.

Hermann's mother looked distressed. "Couldn't you stay another little while?"

"Thank you, no," said Anna and shook Hermann's hand in farewell.

The mother brought her to the door of the flat. There she said, "You know, our pet is an only child."

"So am I," said Anna.

"Ah, but he was never at playschool," said the mother. "That's why he is a little bit rough on other children."

"I didn't go to playschool either," said Anna, gave the mother her hand and ran down the stairs. Hermann's mother sighed and looked sadly after her.

Actually Anna could have gone back to school but that would have looked a bit odd. Sore throats don't get better that quickly.

So Anna went home to Papa's flat and wasn't half amazed to find Papa and Mama there. And both were very agitated!

"I was just about to call the police," shouted Papa, "and set up a missing-person search."

"And I've been to the loo four times," cried Mama. "I have a pain in my stomach through worry about you."

Immediately after the headmistress had rung Papa's office he had returned the call and learned that his poor

Anna was very sick and had been sent home. Naturally he had at once raced home and when he discovered that Anna was not there he had rung the studio and alerted Mama. She had immediately abandoned her rehearsal and come roaring home.

"Where were you, you crazy kid?" cried Papa and Mama. "We've been looking everywhere for you. We've been up and down the road to the school from here a good ten times. We even called Franz-Josef."

"I was with Hermann," said Anna. "I paid him a sick visit."

"What on earth did you go to see that horror for?" shouted Papa.

"Because he had something of mine that I definitely had to have back," said Anna. "Super definitely!"

Mama screamed, "So, you've finally snapped? Sick and running all over the place."

"I'm not sick," said Anna. "That's made itself pretty obvious."

"What's so obvious?" said Papa. "Have you a sore throat or have you not a sore throat? Or are you totally round the twist?"

Anna climbed on top of a chair and roared, "Be quiet! *Now*, if you please."

Always when she was being shouted at by Papa or Mama she got on a chair and screamed back at them. She thought that was only fair. When people are slanging one another then they should at least be able to look one another in the eye. To shout down at "little folk" didn't seem to Anna to be much of a trick. As always when Anna let loose from the top of a chair, her papa and mama had to laugh.

"Okay, okay," said Mama, "Miss Daughter has won again!"

"I'm purring again anyway like an old tomcat," said Papa. He lifted Anna down from the chair and gave her a kiss on the tip of her nose—one of the wet kind that Anna couldn't stand.

"So what happens now?" asked Mama. "There doesn't seem much point in bed-rest and hot compresses and vinegar dressings—or is there?"

"God forbid," said Anna. "I am as fit as a fiddle."

"And for such a brat we had to take time off!" cried Papa and Mama.

"Then, please," said Anna, "if you can take time off for a sick Anna then you can surely blow the free time with a healthy Anna."

"And how, pray?" asked Papa.

"And where, pray?" asked Mama.

"It doesn't matter how or where," said Anna. "Let's just play something."

"Happy Families?" asked Papa. He loved Happy Families.

"Memory?" asked Mama. She always won at Memory.

"Parents and Children," said Anna.

Papa and Mama sighed.

Anna pointed to Mama: "You put on an apron and cook for us a bean goulash with Dutch sausage. We have all the ingredients here!"

Anna pointed to Papa: "And you sit in the living-room, read the paper and complain about the government."

Anna pointed to herself: "And I will run between the pair of you and get awfully on your nerves."

"It's a silly game," murmured Mama.

"And I have already criticised the government—at breakfast," murmured Papa.

"But it's my favourite game," said Anna.

"Just this once then," said Papa and Mama, lifting the apron and the paper.

7

Visiting Peter

If Anna hadn't sneezed the elf awake he would have slept for a whole week. Anna did not begrudge him the four days' rest. She wanted in the end to know exactly what the elf had experienced in Hermann's head and find out whether he had discovered why Hermann was such a nasty kid.

"Ye gods," said the sneezed-awake elf, yawning, "inside Herr Mann's skull utter chaos rules. There's jittering and twittering, thunder and lightning, whimpering and growling, gnawing and sawing and squawking. It's impossible to get the total picture. At all events he gives the impression of being really miserable and believes that he must defend himself against the nastiness of others kids."

Anna sighed. Then your whole trouble went for nothing.

"I don't know for sure," said the elf. "At any rate I have tried in general to put things in order in that skull. I tried to reverse the polarity of a pair of contacts and rewire him. We'll have to wait and see if it has helped."

Anna thought, like bricks it has helped! When we were playing Old Maid he was as yucky as ever. Not a bit friendlier than before.

"Well," said the elf, "maybe my rough contriving works slowly at the start. Perhaps the new circuit which I laid is overloaded. Maybe there's a lot of rust to flake off the old one which I mended. Sometimes it takes time. It doesn't happen overnight."

Please God, thought Anna. She hadn't much hope that the elf was right.

"When will Herr Mann be back at school?"

Next Monday, I suppose, thought Anna. His mother was in the school yesterday. She said that Hermann was doing very well but he is still being medically examined. Every day she goes with him to a different doctor, because it just isn't normal for a child suddenly to get such terrible pains in his head, which then vanished.

The elf laughed. "I'm very pleased," he giggled, "that I got out of his head before they began to X-ray him and give him electronic tests."

Would you have been discovered that way? asked Anna.

"I have no idea," said the elf. "I have had no experience of these things and I'm not a bit curious about them."

Then the elf felt tired again. He was just on the point of helping Anna to do her arithmetic homework. But all the time he yawned horribly and just when Anna closed her arithmetic book, he muttered, "I'll just have a quick zizz," and was out for the count before Anna had put the exercise book in her schoolbag.

That suited Anna. As a matter of fact she wanted to visit Peter. It was his birthday. Anna was the only one invited to his party. No one else! Anna was very proud of that. And at a birthday party she could do very well without the elf.

As well as the big brother whose stained trousers and shirts he had to wear Peter had also three sisters, two older and one younger. The little sister was tiny. She lay in a cot, sucked a dummy and didn't manage once to turn from her stomach to lie on her back. She could lift her head just a little and if you held your hand in front of her nose, she spat out the dummy, laughed and grasped the finger with her little hand and held on.

Peter's two big sisters were already so grown-up that they wore lipstick and had red-varnished fingernails. And they had blonde streaks in their brown hair.

Peter's big brother was called Paul and he was eleven years old. He looked very like Peter and he was not so snooty as other eleven-year-old lads who would not play with little six-year-olds.

Peter's mama was a bit fat and very friendly. And a really crazy baker. On Peter's birthday cake there was as a decoration a thumb-sized Peter that she had made herself.

Peter's apartment was not big. There was a living-room in which during the night Peter's mama and papa slept on a pull-out bed. And the baby in the cot. Then there were two tiny rooms—one for the two big sisters and the other for Peter and Paul. In Peter and Paul's room there were bunk beds, two small desks and two easy chairs. There was no room for anything more.

That was why Peter could not have a proper big birthday party. The children would have had no space to play—indeed they would have had no place to sit.

That didn't worry Peter at all. "The important thing is that you are here," he said to Anna, as he sat with her and the sisters at the kitchen table and cut the cake.

"You're surely his first big heart-throb," said one of the big sisters to Anna and since Peter went beetroot in the face at that, the other one said, "Don't blush like that, Peter. Love is nothing to be ashamed of!"

Then Paul asked Anna, "Are you sweet on him too?" Since one should not be embarrassed at love Anna was not at all red in the face but said simply, "Of course!"

Then Peter's mama took two huge bottles of Coke out of the fridge and six glasses off the sideboard and said, "Then let us toast this happy love."

"Our love would be twice as happy," said Peter, "if we could sit beside each other at school."

Anna nodded. "Right!" she said.

Peter's mother handed round the glasses of Coke. "Then you must arrange that!" she said.

"Especially now that creepy Hermann is not there," said Paul. "The seat beside Anna is empty."

"But Hermann's coming back on Monday," said Anna.

"Then he'll have to sit in Peter's place," said one of the big sisters.

"Michi wouldn't like that," said Anna. "He won't sit beside Hermann."

"I know that Michi," said Peter's mama. "He'll be quite happy beside Hermann. He's better able to defend himself against Hermann than you."

"Exactly," said Paul.

"But will the teacher allow that?" asked Anna.

"Just leave that to me," cried Peter. "First thing tomorrow morning I'll ask her. I'll manage it all right."

"And if Peter can't swing it," said Peter's mama, "I'll go to the school and settle it."

She thrust out her fat chest, lifted her arms and tensed

them like a bodybuilder showing off his biceps, made a tough face and spoke: "I can be really very convincing, if the need arises."

Anna was delighted and not only because of the prospect of utterly marvellous mornings sitting beside Peter. She really loved visiting Peter's house. The big sisters, she reckoned, were the nicest young people she knew. She liked the baby too, although up till then she couldn't abide babies.

When Papa fetched her in the evening, Anna asked Peter's mama, "Can I come soon again?"

"Anna!" cried Papa. "Don't be so pushy! That's not proper form."

"Of course, it's proper form!" said Peter's mama to Papa, and to Anna she said, "As far as I'm concerned you can come every day. One more won't make much difference to us."

All the way home Anna told her papa how lovely it had been at Peter's flat. And when she got home she said, "I'd love to have a big family, sisters and brothers and a baby. Then there would always be someone to play with and talk to and have crack."

"Okay," said Papa. "I'll get married again immediately and produce a big family for you."

"You're nuts!" cried Anna. "I don't want only babies. And you can't produce big brothers and sisters for me; that you would have had to do before I came into the world."

"I'll marry at once a woman who already has older children," said Papa. "That way we'll get a crowd."

"A woman who has children as nice as Peter's brothers and sisters, one you will let me vet first!" cried Anna.

"I must get cracking!" said Papa.

"Forget about it," said Anna. "You'd never manage it."

"I can achieve anything I put my mind to," said Papa.

"Don't you dare!" cried Anna, grabbing the red cushion from the sofa and hurling it at his head.

"I was only making fun," said Papa and placed the red cushion back on the sofa.

"And I can't take fun like that," said Anna and ran out of the living-room. Papa followed her.

"Anna," he said, "you have no sense of humour. Absolutely none!"

Anna took her pink satchel, which had been hanging on the hall-stand, and went into her room. He's gone and spoiled the whole lovely day on me, she thought. Marry, get children. Make fun. When it was clearly no joke.

Anna opened the pink satchel, lifted it up and dumped its contents on the floor.

"What are you at now?" asked Papa, standing in the doorway.

"I'm clearing out my schoolbag. Are you blind?"

"Funny way of doing it," said Papa. "Shall I get the vacuum cleaner and give you a hand?"

"Ah, leave me alone," hissed Anna.

"Truly, Anna," said Papa, "I'm not looking for another wife, with or without children. This I swear!" He lifted his right hand and put his index and his middle finger up.

"Cross your heart...?" asked Anna.

"...and hope to die!" said Papa.

"Okay!" Anna beamed at her papa. She bent down and gathered up again all the school stuff that she had strewn about. Papa helped and then sat on Anna's desk and sharpened all her coloured pencils. The whole two dozen. Then he made a new cover for Anna's reader out of shiny red paper. And after that he and Anna made supper. They cooked rice and lean chops, Anna's favourite dish.

As they ate the meal Papa said, "One way or another, the two of us don't do too badly, eh?"

Anna nodded. One way or another, she decided, Papa was right.

8
Enter Alma

It wasn't necessary for Peter's mama to come to the school and use her powers of persuasion. Peter managed things all on his own.

"It wasn't at all difficult," he said laughing, when he had sat down beside Anna in Hermann's place and stuck his school stuff into the desk. "I didn't have to talk much to the teacher; she agreed immediately. It was stupid of me not to do it long ago."

In all probability the teacher would not have been so agreeable had she realised what a chain reaction it was going to cause. Hardly had Peter settled contentedly beside Anna when Michi put in his oar and asked if now Susi could sit beside him in the empty place.

When the teacher gave permission for that, Alexandra, who up till then had sat beside Susi, joined in and asked if Sascha could now sit beside her.

When the teacher allowed that too, Ruth wanted to have Sascha's "old place"; then Angela wanted Ruth's "old place" and so it went on and on until nearly half the class "swapped" and the bell for break rang. At the finish one desk in the first row remained vacant—the one in front of Anna and Peter.

The teacher said, "Hermann then will sit there when he's well again. And Alma will be beside him when she comes back from the Tyrol."

Peter whispered to Anna: "That's great. It will put that obnoxious Hermann in his place. I know Alma. I was in playschool with her. Her teeth are the softest part of her."

Alma had been staying with her aunt in the Tyrol for a couple of weeks, because her parents had been in a car accident and now were lying in plaster in hospital. Alma had to stay in the Tyrol until her parents recovered.

Anna had a bad conscience about Alma. If Peter hadn't his seat beside me, she thought, Alma wouldn't have had to sit beside Hermann the Horror. And she can't do anything about it because she's not here. And no matter how tough she was she'd be no match for Hermann.

Anna resolved, as a way of making it up to her, to be very nice to Alma. She thought, when Alma comes back I'll bring her a nectarine every day. She told me once that nectarines were her favourite fruit. And I'll give her my little green cloth crocodile as a gift. Whether Alma would like the little green cloth crocodile Anna did not know. But she loved it. And to give it away was a real sacrifice. And Anna reckoned that a real sacrifice was the best cure for an uneasy conscience.

When Hermann came back to school on the Monday and discovered that that his place was in the front row he said simply, "It's all the same to me." But it was clear that he was not content. Anna now sat directly behind Hermann. She watched him the whole morning. She wanted to find out whether the elf had been successful in altering things inside Hermann's head.

But that wasn't so easy to determine. On one hand she had to admit that Hermann was sitting quietly in his place. He didn't grouse. He didn't jostle. He didn't sneak to the teacher. He behaved like a normal child.

On the other hand, thought Anna to herself, there was no one sitting beside him today whom he could jostle or about whom he could sneak to the teacher. He had the desk to himself, no alien coloured pencil could roll into his "half" and there was no one who wanted to borrow his eraser. And today no one talked to him and told him that he had a cat, a dog or a remote-controlled motor boat at home. So Hermann could not boast and claim that he had at home three cats, seven dogs and a whole fleet of remote-controlled craft. At playtime Anna thought, right, I'll try an experiment. She took two coloured pencils and jabbed the leads so hard against the desk that they broke. Then she turned to Hermann. "Look, Hermann," she said, showing him the broken pencils. "Can I please borrow your sharpener? I haven't any with me. At home I have ten sharpeners and a sharpening machine."

He'll immediately say, Anna thought, that he has a hundred sharpeners and ten sharpening machines at home.

Hermann said nothing.

He stayed quiet.

So what, thought Anna. So for once he doesn't boast. But he is pushing his sharpener deeper in, the skinflint!

But Anna was wrong. Hermann was taking his sharpener out of his schoolbag. He handed it to her.

"Don't sharpen too much," he said. "Otherwise you'll be left with a stump."

Anna went with the two coloured pencils and the sharpener to the wastepaper basket.

"Now do you see?" said the elf in her head. He was awake all by himself and with never a yawn.

This could be an exception, thought Anna. She sharpened the pencils, went back to Hermann, put the sharpener on his desk and sat down on the empty chair beside him. She sprawled over the desk so that her left elbow stretched across into Hermann's "half."

Hermann looked a bit unfriendly but again he was silent. Only the elf spoke. "Now do you see!"

Anna lifted her left leg and stuck the point of her shoe into Hermann's right calf. "Well, are you better again?" and stabbed him again with the point of her shoe.

Hermann sprang up and cried, "Miss. Please, miss!"

The teacher was sitting at her desk, turning the pages of a book. She lifted her head. "Yes, Hermann?"

Hermann stood with his mouth open. It was obvious: he wanted to complain about Anna but he couldn't manage it.

"Well, Hermann?" asked the teacher.

"Please, miss, Anna…" said Hermann.

"What about Anna?" asked the teacher.

"Please, she has…" said Hermann.

"What has she?" asked the teacher.

"Please, nothing, miss," said Hermann and sat down again.

"Hermann, Hermann," muttered the teacher, shook her head and returned to her book.

Hermann crouched down, still with his mouth open, rubbed the injured calves with both hands, and clearly couldn't grasp what had happened to him.

"Well then," asked the elf very proudly, "how about Herr Mann now? Am I not a passable pole-reverser, modifier and circuit-layer!"

You are, honestly, thought Anna.

"I'm glad you realise it," said the elf. "The likes of us *do* like to be praised now and then."

At that the bell for the end of playtime sounded and Anna returned to her seat beside Peter.

Peter pointed to Hermann. "What was all that about?" he asked. "Can you explain it to me?"

"No, no idea," whispered Anna and was pleased when the teacher clapped her hands and cried, "Right, no more chatting; to work, folks!"

It's not nice to have to lie to your best friend. One always tells the truth to one's best friend. But when the truth is so incredible it's just not possible.

From the next schoolday on Peter had no need to be surprised at Hermann. He was as odious as ever. He jostled, he groused, he boasted and he complained to the teacher about Michi, because he claimed that Michi had stuffed him into the cloakroom. And he announced during break that he was going to fly to Alaska during the summer holidays to hunt polar bears with his uncle.

Only with Anna was Hermann not nasty. To Anna he was friendly and kind and nice, and kept asking her, "Will you come and visit me? To play Old Maid? And you'll get cake too if you come."

And after lessons when the children were putting on

their street shoes and coats in the cloakroom, Hermann kept asking Anna, "Can I leave you home?"

Anna, of course, refused. She said either, "I'm not going home; actually I'm going to Peter's," or "I'm not going home; I'm going to wait at the corner for Mama. And Peter will wait with me!"

For a while Peter was not pleased that Hermann was so friendly with Anna. He noticed it first when Hermann gave Anna a super apple which he had polished on his trousers till it shone. Peter did not like it when Anna took the apple from him. "I wouldn't take anything from that horror, but nothing!"

And when he heard Hermann invite Anna to come and play Old Maid and eat cake, he said to Anna, "You surely aren't going to visit the creep, or are you? If you go I'll be very cross with you. You're my friend. I won't share you with anybody!"

"No way will I go!" said Anna.

"Cross your heart?" asked Peter.

"Cross my heart," said Anna.

"Will you swear it and hope to die?"

"What for?" Anna found this a bit heavy.

"Because I am actually terribly jealous," said Peter.

"Okay, I'll swear it and hope to die," said Anna. She was delighted that Peter was jealous of her. Jealousy, she thought, is surely a sign of great love.

"Definitely not!" the elf in the head put in. "Jealousy is tiresome and stupid and nothing else. And it has nothing to do with love."

Anna thought, Oh, what do you know about love?

"Heaps," said the elf.

You haven't a clue, thought Anna. You are not a man and you're not a woman. And you have no idea about these things.

Then the elf was hurt and did not speak any more.

9

Happy Families

At least three times a week now Anna spent the afternoon at Peter's house. And as time went by she got fonder and fonder of it. She felt very much at home. She was very fond of Peter's father as well. But she saw him only for a half hour before she had to go home. Peter's father was branch manager of a big hardware business. When he came home from work in the evening he used to stretch himself out on the sofa in the living-room. He had thick blue varicose veins in his legs, because of a lot of standing and running about in the hardware store. His legs gave him a lot of trouble. In spite of that he was always in a good mood. "Children, children, come here," he used to shout as he lay on the sofa, "and tell your old father what's happening in the big, wide world."

Then Peter and Paul and the two big sisters would sit on the sofa and tell their father all that had happened. The mother would bring the baby and put in on the father's stomach. The baby liked it there. And even if it had been whimpering and screeching beforehand it always laughed when it was on the father's stomach.

"It's no surprise," said Peter's father. "I give off loving vibes."

Anna had to agree with him. She would have loved to have gone home with Peter every day after school. And Peter's family wouldn't have had the slightest objection. But Anna couldn't do that to her mama. Mama always complained, "Anna, you don't have time for me any more. I have always kept myself free for your afternoons."

Only when she had an afternoon rehearsal or was on tour with the company was Mama pleased that Anna was treated like one of the family at Peter's. She didn't have to pay the costly Franz-Josef any more. And she didn't have to listen any more to Anna's complaints when Liesl or some other friend had to be got to look after her.

Mama wanted Anna to go to Peter's house only on the afternoons when she couldn't take Anna herself. Anna objected to that. "Look, that's far too little for me," she said to her mama. "Then I'd see Peter far too seldom."

"Well, as it is now, I see you far too seldom," moaned her mama.

"But I'm so fond of Peter," said Anna, "that mornings aren't enough at all."

"And are you not fond of me?" asked Mama looking very sad.

"Don't talk silly!" shouted Anna. "That's completely different!"

"It's not a bit different!" cried Mama. "How much of your love do I have, if you have no time for me?"

Anna had no answer to that but thankfully the elf was awake and he said, "That make's me want to puke—it's pure blackmail!"

So Anna said to her mother, "You know, that makes me want to puke—it's pure blackmail!"

"What?" asked Mama.

"Just that!" murmured Anna because again she couldn't think of an answer. But the elf in the head said, "If she hadn't got divorced and if she hadn't such a stupid job, she could see you quite often enough."

So Anna added to her "Just that" with "If you hadn't got divorced and hadn't such a stupid job, then you could see me quite often enough."

And now it was Mama who had no answer. And because she had no elf in her head to prompt her, she just murmured, "Anna, oh, Anna," and looked at her out of sad doggy eyes.

If the elf had not been there the sad doggy eyes would have surely made a deep impression on Anna. It was hard for Anna to resist Mama when she was sad. Anna wanted to promise her Mama that from now on she would again have time for her much oftener but the elf whispered, "One cannot help noting that the woman is an actress. Don't fall for it! If she is honest, she can see you oftener without depriving you of your afternoons with Peter."

So Anna did not fall for it and just looked at the floor so that she didn't have to look at the sad doggy eyes. Mama realised that the sad doggy look wasn't working today and said at length, "Okay, if there's nothing else for it, I'll apply to your papa for more weekends with you. That he'll have to agree to. The time spent with Peter mustn't be taken only from my time with you; your father too must give up some of his time with you."

"That's great by me," said Anna. "Arrange it to suit yourselves!"

And the elf said, "Now do you see? You must stand up for yourself; otherwise you always end up the fall guy."

That very same evening Mama phoned Anna's papa.

They squabbled for rather a long time on the phone.

He couldn't see why the mama should from now on be entitled to more weekend time with Anna. "One weekend with you, one with me," he roared into the receiver, "that's what was agreed and that's the way it will stay. That's that!"

What her mama answered to this Anna couldn't, of course, understand but it was certainly not friendly. Papa shouted, "Don't use that tone of voice with me! Otherwise this conversation ends now!" and "Control yourself!" and "I won't allow you to insult me any further!"

Then Papa began to lose the head. "You are and always were a ludicrous person," he thundered. And "What a hysterical woman!" and "Stop screeching like a circular saw; my ears are falling off me!"

Anna stood at the living-room door and tried to stop herself from crying but she was too miserable.

"He's just as bad as your mama," said the elf. "The two of them are so obdurate that they can't be reasonable."

Anna nodded and the elf yawned and muttered, "I'm gong to have a quick kip now. This nasty telephone call has worn me out. I won't listen to another word of it."

You're a lot of help, thought Anna.

"That's not fair." The elf yawned again. "Since coming to live with you I've been awake far, far oftener than before. I have never been so wide awake in all my life as I have been with you. I can't hack it any more." And the guy was snoring again.

Anna sneezed. Once, twice, three times. The elf didn't stir. Anna sneezed a further three times. The elf groaned, "I want to sleep!"

Anna sneezed three *more* times. The elf wailed, "Give

me peace. Otherwise I'll fall apart."

Nevertheless Anna continued to sneeze, without a break, millions of times. As if she had a bag of pepper up her nose. She felt awfully miserable and dispirited. And what was the good of having an elf in the head if he did not stand by her in times of despair!

Such a bighead, thought Anna. Think only of yourself. Don't notice that I am sorely in need of comfort.

The the elf screeched, "You'll get no comfort while this is going on. This is what you must do: end this stupid telephone call. You're not a ping-pong ball that those two apes can toss between them whenever they take the notion. Tell them that. Don't stand around waiting for comfort."

Anna took a deep breath and went over to her Papa. She plucked him by the pullover. "Papa!" she said.

Papa continued to rage into the telephone and paid no attention to Anna. Anna pulled harder on his pullover and cried, "Papa, listen to me!"

Her Papa made no move to turn to her and scolded further into the phone.

Anna released her grip on the pullover, pummelled her Papa with both fists on the bottom and howled, "Listen to me; listen to me now! I will not allow you to quarrel so foully with my mama."

Shocked, Papa laid the receiver to one side and turned to Anna.

"I'm not a ping-pong ball," Anna screamed. "You two apes are not going to toss me between you whenever you feel like it."

The elf whispered, "Tell him that you will go at weekends to Peter if they can't agree."

"And if you two can't agree, then from now on I will spend the weekends as well with Peter."

Anna tore the receiver from Papa's hand and screamed into it, "Did you hear that, Mama?"

"Of course, darling, it was loud enough!"

Anna pressed the receiver into Papa's hand again and stalked into her room and slammed the door behind her.

"Well, did I do it right?" she asked the elf.

"You were magic," said the elf yawning

Okay, thought Anna, off you go to sleep. I don't want you falling apart on me.

The elf didn't answer. He was snoring. It seemed to Anna that the snores were very contented.

Hardly ten minutes later Papa came into Anna's room. "Anna," he said, "your mama and I have a proposal to make."

"What is is?" asked Anna.

"So that neither Mama nor I gets a raw deal, "said Papa, "we are going to spend the weekends together, the three of us. As Parents and Children. It's your favourite game."

"Very sensible!" said Anna.

"Okay," said Papa. "Then I'll let your mama know that you agree." Papa went into the living-room to the telephone. Anna heard him sigh. He sighed very deeply. Anna thought: why does he sigh like that? Is it the worst thing in his life to have to spend weekends with Mama? He'll get used to it. And if he doesn't get used to it, well, there's nothing to be done.

Anna had long ago realised that in "separated families," problems can never be solved to everyone's satisfaction.

10

Scarlet Fever

The new weekend solution pleased Anna because Anna was happy to be a "normal" child and a "normal" child had simply a mama and a papa at weekends and had no need to distinguish between a Papa-Sunday and a Mama-Sunday.

But the Papa-and-Mama weekends had a further advantage. When Anna was with her mama and papa at a weekend, she did not have to deal with either Oskar or Karla.

Karla was a "dear friend" of Papa. She had been so for a year. Before that she was merely a colleague at the office. Karla always came on Sundays to visit papa and was always one of the party when Anna and her papa went to the zoo or went on a trip or went to a restaurant for a meal. And when Anna and Papa arranged to spend the Sunday at home then Karla would arrive with a grip full of meat and vegetables and flour and butter and chocolate, and cook in Papa's flat a four-course Sunday lunch.

Oskar was a "dear friend" of Mama and always visited Mama when Anna was spending the weekend with her. If Anna went with Mama to have an ice cream or to the cinema or to the park, he came with them.

Oskar and Karla were very friendly and kind to Anna. Nevertheless she couldn't stick them all that much. She couldn't abide Oskar since the time the landlady of Mama's house had said to her, "Well, Anna, what do you think? Wouldn't Mr Oskar be a nice papa for you?"

Anna couldn't stick Karla ever since Michi had asked her, "Tell me, Anna, that woman who was with you and your father at the pool yesterday, is she going to be your new mama?"

Anna didn't want either a new papa or a new mama. Normal children did not have two of each!

Peter could not understand that. He said, "Why ever not? If this Karla and this Oskar are so sweet to you, that's fine! You'll be loved double. That can't be bad!"

Paul considered two pairs of parents a bit of all right. "No, listen," he said, "it's a double whammy! You'll get pocket-money twice, birthday presents twice and Christmas presents twice!"

And Peter's two big sisters said, "And if one mama and papa are nasty to you, you have always another papa and mama who'll be nice to you!'

Peter's mama understood Anna. She said to Peter and Paul and the two big sisters, "You are crazy! You have no idea!"

And Peter's papa said too, "Anna, don't take these twits seriously. They know nothing about life!"

Sometimes Anna thought, if Peter's papa would marry my mama and Peter's mama would marry my papa, I'd have no objection, because then we would have one big, happy family. Before she fell asleep she painted a mental picture of how it would be: they'd all live in a big house.

In a big house with a garden behind. And they'd have a giant living-room in which they'd all sit together in the evenings and have fun.

When Anna used to imagine this and the elf was awake he would tease her about it. "Such a silly idea," he snickered.

Anna used to have the odd row with the elf. Mostly the row would begin in school. And Hermann was always the cause. The elf was in fact tremendously proud that he had rearranged things so successfully in "Herr Mann's" head. He continually praised his headwork.

I see no sign of success, thought Anna, just when Hermann had peached to the teacher about Michi. And all because Michi had taken a bite of bread and butter during the lesson!

"But he is very nice to you," said the elf. "He's no longer horrible to you in any way since I was in his head."

And when Hermann once gave Anna three cherries the elf fell into raptures. "Isn't that gas?" he shouted. "He hands you cherries! My doing! Congratulate me!"

Anna decided it was too much to expect her to congratulate the elf for three miserable cherries. She thought: Hermann only gave them to me because they were maggoty. (That was a lie! The three cherries were certainly not maggoty.)

The elf snarled. "Tut-tut! Shame on you! You're a mean strap. You're always rotten to Herr Mann."

I don't like him at all, thought Anna. No one could like him.

The elf could not agree to that. "Surely," he maintained, "if he likes you you must like him!"

And whenever Hermann invited Anna to his house to

play Old Maid and eat cake the elf always wanted Anna to accept. "Do it to please him," he cried. "Why won't you visit him? Especially when he is so fond of you? Must you always run to Peter? A bit of a change couldn't harm us!"

I don't want to go, thought Anna.

"But I do!" shouted the elf. "But I can't go except in your head, since I'm in here. In fact I live as a tenant here and a tenant has no rights."

Since the elf would not leave her alone, Anna promised him that she would visit Hermann. I'll do it for your sake, she thought. But only once! One single time. And after an hour I'm leaving. Understood?

"Understood!" said the elf.

Still Anna postponed the visit to Hermann from one week to the next. This was the problem: Peter was always with Anna in the school. He never budged from her side. And he was always about when Hermann asked Anna, "When are you coming to visit me?"

Then Peter would look hopping mad and whisper to Anna, "Do you really want to go with that dope?"

Anna did not risk accepting Hermann's invitation in front of Peter. She didn't want a row with Peter because of Hermann.

You must see that, explained Anna to the elf. How shall I explain to Peter that I am visiting Hermann. Peter doesn't know that you exist. So he will think that I like Hermann. And he doesn't want me to like anybody apart from him!

Each day Anna explained this to the elf but the elf would not see it. Then one day he was really fed up and he roared, "I've put up with this nonsense long enough.

I'm going to sleep now and I won't wake up again until you are visiting Herr Mann. And I swear to you that if I do wake up and you are not in Hermann's on a visit, then I'm pulling out, I'll find another head to live in! One that will grant me from time to time a tiny little request."

Anna was frightened and shocked. Elf, dear elf, she thought, you're only joking.

The elf did not answer. Anna did not believe that he was asleep. This time he is in earnest. Dead, dead earnest!

During the next few days Anna hardly dared to think, in case she should waken the elf. So every sneeze, even the slightest, she smothered. She was in a terrible state. She could see no solution to her problem. If she visited Hermann Peter would be angry with her; if she didn't visit Hermann the elf would finish with her head.

If Paul had not caught scarlet fever, Anna could not have solved her difficult problem.

When a child catches scarlet fever, clearly his brothers and sisters must stay away from school because scarlet fever is very infectious. The brothers and sisters could become infected and give it to the other children in the school. So because Paul had got scarlet fever Peter wasn't allowed to go to school either—even though he was as healthy as a trout. And Anna wasn't allowed to visit him. She was allowed only to telephone. It was awful for Anna. She felt so much at home when she was at Peter's! Now she had to stay every afternoon in her mama's flat again and it felt almost as if it was a foreign land.

After a week of unrelieved Mama-afternoons and a Mama-and-Papa weekend, as Anna lay in bed on Sunday evening it suddenly hit her: actually I could now grant the elf's silly request. I could visit Hermann tomorrow afternoon. Mama has another rehearsal for a radio play. And Franz-Josef has no time for me. If I go home with Hermann after school I'll escape an afternoon with stupid Liesl. And Peter won't be aware that I am with Hermann.

Anna sneezed all the way to the supermarket house. Hermann didn't like that. "Have you got a cold?" he asked.

"A slight one," said Anna, grinning, and kept on sneezing.

"Please don't sneeze in my direction," said Hermann. "Otherwise I'll catch the cold; I'm very prone to them."

"Aaaah, excuse me," sneezed Anna right in Hermann's face. He had till then been very close beside her but now he jumped a pace to the side and walked at a distance of

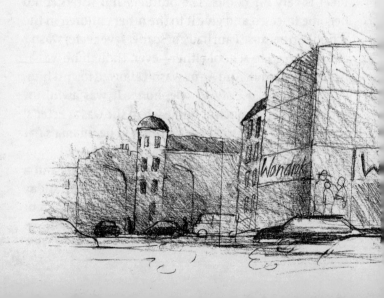

a metre from her.

Just immediately outside the supermarket Anna at last sneezed the elf awake.

"It's about time too that you're doing what I want," said the elf.

What do you mean! thought Anna; it was only yesterday that you threatened me with leaving. Anna reckoned that it was easy to deceive someone who had no idea of time. But it's not so easy to deceive someone who sits inside your head!

"Don't lie," said the elf.

How do you know that I am lying? thought Anna.

"Always when you are lying," said the elf, "there's a kind of noise. It's like a little fart but it does not stink!"

Stupid, thought Anna.

"And as well," said the elf, "I was awake a couple of times but I waited till now. One mustn't carry out every threat. I was extremely reluctant to move out. Why should I do anything I don't want to do?"

On the way up the stairs Hermann stuck very close to Anna again. She had stopped sneezing!

At the door of Hermann's flat the elf said, "I hope you'll be nice and friendly to Herr Mann. He is obviously fond of you. And it's bad to love and not be loved in return. And I consider myself responsible in this affair. Because I arranged this love for you."

Anna did not ask the elf any more about what he, for goodness' sake, had arranged, because Hermann had rung the flat doorbell and his mother flung the door open and chattered like a magpie. She took the satchel off Anna's shoulder and the cap from her head. She unbuttoned her jacket and took it off, and announced that she was so very pleased to see Anna again and that now Anna must come much, much, much oftener and that there was stuffed ham for lunch and did Anna like it? And would she like ice cream or blancmange or both afterwards, and how was she at homework, did she do it quickly or was she slow and would she do it along with Hermann or wait till evening and do it at home?

Anna was completely fogged by the chatter and let herself be led into the living-room and pushed towards a chair by Hermann's mother. She sat down on the chair and thought: with a mother like that the child *has* to be nuts.

11

Hermann Loves Anna!

It was only while they were eating the stuffed ham and Hermann's mother was chewing and bolting down the food and wasn't able to gabble so much, that Anna quizzed the elf about what he meant by "love" and "arranged."

And while Hermann's mother dished up both blancmange and ice cream and Hermann demanded whipped cream as well, the elf explained to Anna what he had meant. He said, "It's quite clear. He has thumped you and pinched you and grassed on you. And I have been inside him to discover why he behaves like that. But in the mad confusion of his brain, in the whole flashing and growling and roaring, I wasn't able to work out exactly why he behaved as he did. To make a proper diagnosis one would have to stay in him for a year. But one thing is obvious. If someone loves someone else then he does not punch him or nip him or grass on him. And is surely not mean to him. So I have discovered two spots in his brain, one tiny, the other rather bigger..." The elf stopped speaking.

Talk on, thought Anna impatiently.

"And it seemed to me I could try..." said the elf.

What have you tried? Anna was growing steadily more impatient.

"Well, between the tiny spot and the somewhat larger spot I devised a connection," said the elf, "and I cleared up all the junk that lay around, loosened what was too tight, and diverted what was causing obstruction!" The elf's voice got impatient. "But I have already explained this to you from beginning to end."

Anna thought, he said nothing about a tiny spot and a somewhat bigger spot.

"Didn't I?" asked the dwarf acting the innocent. "Well then, I completely forgot it!"

Now at last will you tell me what these spots are? thought Anna.

"Ah, that's simple enough," said the elf. "The tiny spot was where he had stored *Anna* and the somewhat larger spot was where he had stored *Love*.

I'm going out of my mind, thought Anna.

"So you must be very nice to him," said the elf. "It would be unfair for me to have connected him to a love and for him to get nothing back. That would be unrequited love and unrequited love is a tragedy. And I am not allowed to start up a tragedy inside a head."

You should have asked me first, thought Anna, whether I agreed to it.

"How, pray?" cried the elf. "The idea struck me only when I was already inside Hermann's head. Should I perhaps have run out again and into your head and raced from your head yet again into his? I'm no marathon runner. And you know well that I can't take fresh air. I get quite a serious attack of oxygen poisoning if I as much as look out of your ear."

But you can't simply *compel* me to fall in love, thought Anna. And suddenly a terrible thought flashed through her head: Could the elf not do that? Who was to stop him monkeying about in her head and perhaps cut through the connection between *Peter* and *Love* and re-route it to Herr Mann?

"On my word of honour, I wouldn't do the like of that," cried the elf indignantly. "That is definitely not possible because you are aware that I am inside you. It's only inside heads that don't know about me that I can turn things upside down."

Nevertheless, Anna was not certain that the elf was telling her the strict truth.

"I find it very shabby," said the elf, "that you don't trust me."

Why should I? thought Anna. For one thing is certain. You always know what I'm thinking and I never know what you're thinking. I never know exactly when you are asleep and when you are awake. For that matter your snoring could be just a trick. One can snore when one is awake!

The elf was raging, really annoyed. "I'll never utter a word to you again," he said. "Not a single word."

Because you don't want to hear the truth, thought Anna. Because I'm clearly in the right and you don't want to admit it.

Then the elf said a bit more. He spoke in a bitterly cross voice: "I can't help it if you're too stupid to understand my thoughts. Maybe it's my fault that you're such a dim twit."

Now Anna was angry, really mad. I'll never speak to you again, thought she. Not for as long as I live! You can pull out from me and go to blazes.

Anna was properly sick after wolfing down the blancmagne-ice-cream-whipped-cream dessert. Whether she simply had gorged herself or it was the row with the elf that caused it she didn't know. She wanted desperately to be home—in Papa's flat. Her greatest wish at that moment was to be totally alone, without having to see anyone. But in the first place, Papa did not like it when Anna was home alone. Anna is still far too small, he always said, to be at home alone at all. And secondly, she dreaded a flood of chat from Hermann's mother when she realised that Anna no longer wanted to stay with her "dotey." So Anna went with Hermann into the playroom. She played for a bit with the motor racetrack. She played Old Maid too. Hermann behaved nicely. When he had only two cards left in his hand and Anna picked the one which wasn't the Old Maid he no longer glowered at her, nor was so rude as to hold on to it and shout, "I won't let it go."

Anna tried the whole afternoon to convince the dwarf and herself that there was no working connection in Hermann's head that led from *Anna* to *Love*. She was mean to Hermann. She complained at every opportunity. She asked, "Where is this St Bernard you told us about? Where is your house with the ten rooms? Do you keep it in the cellar?" And she looked at the car track and said with a smirk, "We're missing a good sixty-five metres. When is it coming?"

Hermann turned beetroot and stared at the floor. This annoyed Anna. She wished he would pinch, thump, go moaning to his mother about her.

Then the elf would have seen that Hermann did not

fancy her at all. And he could not have required that Anna love Hermann. And the stupid row would be finished.

But Hermann did not do Anna that favour. Quite the opposite. Indeed he gave Anna the Matchbox car that his uncle had given him only a few days before. He also gave her a ball-point that could write in lilac. Not once when Anna trod on his toes did he protest. He just cried, "Oh dear!" And that, as Anna had to admit, any other kid would certainly have done. Even Peter! Then just before Anna went home, Hermann said to her, "Look, I'd really, really like to sit beside you again. And I'll never behave so badly ever again, I promise."

Anna arrived home in an utterly miserable and grumpy mood. And Papa made her even more miserable and grumpy. He wanted to know exactly why Anna had spent the afternoon at Hermann's. Was it that she no longer regarded him as a total creep? Had she concluded a friendship pact with him? And what was Peter going to say about that? Had she not told him that Peter was a jealous guy?

Papa couldn't help noticing that Anna did not wish to speak about Hermann. And when Anna told him so, he would not hold his tongue. He wanted then to know why she didn't want to talk about Hermann.

"I see that my dear child has a problem. One should discuss problems. Staying miserably silent and glaring grumpily about achieves nothing!"

"Don't be so interfering," shouted Anna.

"You always want me to tell you everything," cried Papa.

"And you don't!" Anna retorted.

"Only because you wouldn't understand," cried Papa.

"Well, I too have things that about which you understand nothing!" screamed Anna.

"Maybe I understand them, nevertheless," said Papa. "For that is the difference between us. You are not grown up yet. And you don't know everything about this growing-up business. But I was a kid too. It follows that I understand everything about being a kid!"

"Right then," said Anna and considered how she might explain her problems to Papa, without mentioning the elf.

"Well, recently Hermann has fallen in love with me," began Anna.

"Ah ha," said Papa. That he seemed to understand.

"But of course I don't love him," Anna continued.

"You bet!" said Papa. That too he seemed to grasp.

"And there's someone," Anna sighed deeply, "who insists that it is my duty to love Hermann, and if I don't do that he will never speak to me again."

"What a dope!" said Papa.

"Right on," said Anna.

"Well, I reckon," said Papa, "that if a twit doesn't want to talk to me, it's no big deal!"

Anna had the suspicion that the elf could be awake and she had no wish to eat humble pie before that guy! So she said, "You're absolutely right. The twit can go and jump!"

Anna acted as if things were all right with her again. She helped Papa cook the evening meal. She peeled the potatoes, sliced the dill up very thin. She set the table as well. But she did not feel much like eating. A few bites made her feel sick.

"It's because I ate so much at Hermann's at midday," she fibbed to Papa.

Then Anna went and lay down on her bed and because it was quiet as a mouse in the room she heard the elf in the head gently snoring.

Mean bastard, she thought. Only a rough insensitive hound could sleep so peacefully after such a mega-fight. That stupid wrinkly elf doesn't care a damn about how I'm doing. He is far more concerned about Hermann than about me. Let him leave me. Let him go and live in Hermann's blockhead skull!

In the middle of the night Anna woke. This had never happened to her before. Usually she slept like a marmot in winter. She lay in the pitch dark, tossed from lying on her back to her stomach and from her stomach to her back and again to her stomach. She heard the clock in the church tower strike midnight, she heard a drunk singing in the street and a car round the corner with squealing tyres. But she heard no snoring from the dwarf. She thought, I believe that the elf has wakened me.

"Right," said the elf, "because I don't want to be cross with you any more. I can't bear that."

Me neither, thought Anna.

"And there's only one solution," sighed the elf. "I must get into the head of Herr Mann once more and detach the connection. But that is definitely the last time I will venture into the open air."

You are a super elf, thought Anna.

Then Anna and the dwarf yawned in unison three times three and by the ninth yawn both had fallen fast asleep.

12

Peter Finds Out

It was not nearly as simple as the elf had thought to do the repairs in Hermann's head. On the first day the elf wanted to get inside Hermann he came to school with cotton wool in his ears.

"I have the wool in," he told Anna, "because there is such a wind today. Otherwise I'd get earache."

"But there's no wind in the classroom," said Anna, grabbing Hermann by the ear and wanting to pull out the cotton wool.

"Leave it alone!" shouted Hermann.

The elf shouted too, "Leave it alone!" He meant that it was pointless. "If he were to put in fresh wool while I was inside his head I'd be imprisoned. We'll postpone the business, preferably till the next calm day!"

The next windless day came three days later and Hermann appeared with no plugs in his ears. But also on that day Alma came back to school for the first time and sat beside Hermann. Alma had been so long in the Tyrol that she had forgotten what an oddball Hermann was. She made no complaint about her new place. She wasn't annoyed either when Hermann rammed her in the ribs with his elbow because she had put down one of her coloured pencils in his "half." She stamped very heavily on his toes and said, "Behave yourself, you warthog!"

And during break she snatched Hermann's sausage sandwich and took three big bites out of it, not bothering about the racket Hermann made. Laughing and munching she said, "Cool it, old sport, you'll not die of starvation." And when Susi then announced that she got thirty pence pocket money every week and Hermann boasted that he got five pounds pocket money, Alma stuck out her hand at Hermann and said, "If you have all that money, cough up a quid; I get no pocket money at all!"

Anna thought, Alma knows exactly how to handle Hermann.

"I agree," said the elf. "So I'll not snip off the lead in Hermann's head but transpose it from *Anna* to *Alma*."

Anna snickered. A burning love for Alma she would not begrudge Hermann the Fink.

"But we must still wait a day or two," said the elf. "*Alma* must be properly fed in to his brain!"

The elf decided that the following Monday should be the time to begin. But he couldn't start the operation during the first lesson because they had PE and the time when Hermann was jumping about in the gym was bad for switching heads. "You have no idea," he said, "how very delicate these things are. All it needs is the slightest vibration for everything to go *phut*!"

At playtime Anna did everything she could to stick close to Hermann so that the elf could climb across. But Hermann had started a fight with Alma and she had given him a clip on the ear. Now the pair of them were scrapping and only stopped their fight just as the bell rang for the end of break. The following break lasted only five minutes. Five minutes wasn't enough for the elf's operation.

For a whole fortnight Anna and the elf tried the head-switch. But something prevented it every day. Once the dwarf was poised on Anna's outer ear and then Hermann ran to the loo. Once the elf had got as far as Anna's shoulder and was ready to jump but Susi pushed between Anna and Hermann and told Anna that her mama was going to have another baby and that she wasn't all that happy about it.

The only result of all these attempts at transfer was that now all the children in the class believed that Anna was Hermann's sweetheart—because Anna was always by his side.

"It won't work in school," said the elf finally. "You'll have to visit him at home."

Anna agreed with him and said to Hermann, "If you like, I'll come with you tomorrow afternoon."

"That's magic!" said Hermann, beaming from ear to ear.

Then Alma called, "I'll come too, Hermann."

"I certainly didn't invite you," said Hermann.

"I'll come without an invitation," said Alma agreeably.

The afternoon at Hermann's with Alma there was very jolly. True, Hermann was not so friendly to Alma but Alma did not take offence. She just growled, "Be quiet, you old skunk," when he behaved badly.

Yet the dwarf's head exchange did not happen. This time it was his fault. "I don't feel right," he yawned. "No wonder. I've been awake for yonks. I'm overextended. If I should go out now the fresh air would topple me." Then he yawned and fell asleep. Anna made no attempt to wake him. She knew already that an elf who had only with great difficulty been sneezed awake should not be considered for the task.

On the last schoolday of that week the elf woke himself. "I have dreamed up this fantastic idea," he said. "Go with Herr Mann to the pictures. There he will be sitting for two hours beside you in the dark. Then I can work with his connections in perfect peace."

So Anna invited Hermann to the pictures, on the Saturday afternoon. Alma heard about it and cried, "Fine. I'll come too."

"You're not invited," groused Hermann.

"Do come," said Anna. "A threesome is far better crack anyway."

Mama and Papa were quite astonished that on her family weekend Anna had planned a Saturday afternoon visit to the cinema in the company of Hermann and Alma.

"Why go with the creep?" asked Mama. And Papa muttered, "I thought that this problem was being dealt with."

Because Papa had only muttered and had not actually asked a question Anna did not think she was required to answer.

Laurel and Hardy in the Foreign Legion was the film Anna picked from the programme in the paper.

Papa, Mama and Anna first drove in Papa's car to Alma's house and brought her with them. Then they drove to the supermarket building. Hermann was waiting there at the main door. Anxiously Anna studied Hermann—because there was a bit of a wind blowing.

But, thank heavens, Hermann had no wool in his ears.

Papa and Mama weren't keen on Laurel and Hardy. They bought three tickets at the desk and slipped them into Anna's hand. "We'll have a seat in the café next door," said Papa

"When the movie is over, come and get us," said Mama.

In the cinema Hermann sat down between Anna and Alma. Directly the lights went down, the elf said, "Here goes. Keep your fingers crossed for me!"

What will I do if he moans and girns again? thought Anna.

"Laugh out loud," said the elf. After all you're sitting in a cinema at a funny picture. Make more noise with your laughing than he does with his groans and girning!"

Anna felt a little tickle in her ear. She leant closer to Hermann and said quietly, "May I lean myself against you? I'll see much better."

"Yes, lean away," said Hermann.

In front of them on the screen Laurel and Hardy were squabbling. The audience laughed. Anna squinted at Hermann's shoulder. She couldn't see the elf. It was too dark for that. But Hermann neither groaned nor girned. He just watched the screen and giggled.

Anna was very relieved. So far so good, she thought. Scarcely had she had the thought when she felt again the gentle tickle in her ear and immediately the elf screeched, "Damn and blast! What an incredible mess!"

What's wrong? asked Anna frightened.

"He has his ears full of eardrops," groaned the elf. "Full of greasy eardrops. I nearly slipped inside and drowned in oil." The elf wheezed. "That would have been the finish of me!"

The elf shuddered with horror so much that Anna became very dizzy.

Stop it, she thought, I can't stand this.

"Sorry," said the elf and kept still. But he sighed in great misery.

Don't be so dramatic, thought Anna. Some time in the future Hermann won't have drops in his ear. And then you can snip the connection. In a couple of days the guy will be able to go on living without being loved.

"You don't get it at all!" yelled the elf. "You are really dim! Truly!" Then he said no more. Whether he was asleep or offended or simply watching Laurel and Hardy, Anna didn't know.

After the film Anna, Alma and Hermann collected Mama and Papa from the café.

On the way home after Hermann and Alma had been deposited, Mama said, "You know, Hermann doesn't seem to be such a horror," and Papa said, "He seemed very mannerly, that lad. And he's certainly handsome."

Shortly before six o'clock Papa, Mama and Anna arrived at Papa's flat. Papa and Mama went into the living-room. Mama had brought a bundle of paper-work with her. She had to fill up her tax form and hadn't a clue how to go about it. Papa had promised to help her.

Anna sat in the hall by the telephone. Exactly at six each evening she and Peter spoke on the phone. One day she rang Peter, the next day Peter rang her. Today was Peter's turn.

It got to five past six, then ten past six but the phone did not ring. So Anna rang Peter. One of the big sisters answered. "Peter doesn't want to talk to you," she said.

Anna was so shocked that she couldn't ask why Peter did not want to speak to her. However, the big sister explained it to her. "Michi rang him today," she said, "and told him that you were now Hermann's sweetheart and that you went to the pictures with him today. We all told him that it was nonsense." The big sister stopped talking. She appeared to be waiting for an explanation from Anna. When none came she asked, "Or is that the case?"

Anna spoke in a trembling voice, "It is like that and yet it's not like that."

The big sister sighed and said, "Well, that's something you'll have to sort out between you."

"How?" Anna was sobbing now. "When he won't speak to me?"

"He'll be coming back to school on Monday," said the big sister. "The infection period is past. Since he sits beside you he'll certainly have to listen to you." Then she added, "Anna, don't cry on account of such a jealous dimwit."

Anna replaced the receiver and howled her head off. She grizzled so loud that Papa and Mama heard her from the living-room. They hurried into the hallway and asked what, in heaven's name, was the matter. But more than "I'm so unhappy, so terribly unhappy" they could not get out of her.

13

Mama and Papa Meet the Elf

Anna was really confused when she woke on Sunday morning. The easy chair which could be made into a makeshift bed stood unfolded beside her bed. On it Mama lay asleep. She was wearing a pair of Papa's pyjamas and was covered with the tartan travelling rug. Since Mama left after the divorce she had never stayed the night in Papa's flat.

"It was on your account she slept there," said the elf. He didn't yawn, so he must have been awake for ages.

Why on my account? thought Anna.

"Why, because of the performance you put on," said the elf.

Anna tried to recall the previous evening. There was the terrible telephone call with Peter's sister; then she had wept and Mama and Papa had tried to console her. And what then?

"Wept is an understatement," said the elf. "You howled like a pack of hungry wolves and the sobbing made you shake as if you were handling a pneumatic drill. And at least half gallon of tears ran down your cheeks."

Well, thought Anna, that's how it is with a broken heart.

"All through your sleep you shook and jittered. That's why your mama decided that she must sit up with you."

That was kind of Mama, thought Anna.

"Indeed," said the elf, "humans console each other when they are miserable."

That's the way it should be, thought Anna.

"But not a being cares about my misery!" said the elf. "And I'm a lot more miserable than you."

He's exaggerating again, thought Anna.

"I'm not exaggerating at all," cried the elf. "I'm in it as never before."

How? thought Anna.

"Must I explain it to you a hundred times?" rasped the elf. "My greatest responsibility is to be certain I do no damage inside a skull. And I have caused Hermann to fall in love with you and you don't love him back. So he has been damaged. And because of the stupid ear oil I can't undo that damage."

Well, that's true, thought Anna. But it's no worse now than ever it was.

"I'm really up the creek," said the elf. "I've messed up, and when one of us has messed up he dries up and wrinkles and shrinks to a tiny hard dot that could easily pass for a nit."

"No!" Anna was so dismayed that she shouted aloud. That woke her mama. She sat up and looked at Anna. But Anna acted as if she were still asleep and turned to the wall. At the moment she had no time for her mother! Just now the elf was more important.

Mama rose from the chair-bed and tiptoed out of the room. Anna stared at the wallpaper border on the wall behind the bed. She thought, the elf is going to shrink, the elf is going to dry up, the elf is going to end up as a nit. It mustn't happen. One has to do something to prevent it!

"But what?" The elf's voice sounded hopeless.

I'm going to have to love Hermann, thought Anna. For the elf I'd do anything.

"You're a heroine!" he sniffled, apparently drawing the tear-snot up through his nose.

Okay, I'll do what is necessary, thought Anna. Already she felt a little bit like a heroine. And in case she too should begin to sniffle from sheer self-pity, she leapt from the bed.

In the hallway Anna met Papa. "Good morning, my darling," said Papa looking at her with X-ray eyes.

"Good morning," murmured Anna and ran into the kitchen. Mama was there. She said, "Good morning, darling," and also looked at her with X-ray eyes.

Anna thought: Right away she'll pester the life out of me with questions about yesterday evening.

But Mama only asked whether Anna wanted cocoa or coffee. "Cocoa," said Anna and sat down at the kitchen table. Then Papa came and sat beside Anna. Mama gave him coffee. Anna got her cocoa and crunchy toast. She drank the cocoa and nibbled at the toast. The X-ray looks of Mama and Papa were tiresome. She thought, they are looking at me as if I'd grown another head overnight.

"They just think you're an eejit," said the elf.

Anna looked Papa and Mama in the eye and cried, "I am no kind of an eejit!"

"No one said you were," said Papa with a very gentle voice.

"Only when you cry for hours," said Mama in a still gentler voice.

"And don't tell us why," began Papa.

"So that we worry," said Mama finishing the sentence.

And the elf said, "Okay, tell them what's wrong. They think you're an eejit already. So it can't get any worse."

Anna nodded, then said to her mama and papa, "Well, I have an elf in my head."

Papa, who was taking a drink of his coffee, choked, coughed and spat out coffee. Coughing and spluttering he yelled, "Now the nuttiness is starting again!"

Anna ignored Papa's objection. "And my elf," she said, "was in Hermann's head and set up a link between me and *Love*. And if I don't love Hermann he'll turn into a nit. But if I love Hermann, Peter will never more be friends with me!"

Papa let his coffee-cup fall. It smashed into three large pieces. Dark brown liquid flooded the table and soaked the legs of Mama's pyjamas.

"And now I'd like to know," said Anna, "how little a person need love for it still to count as *love*."

Anna waited for an answer. But Papa continued to cough and splutter and Mama wiped the brown muck off her legs.

"Naturally they don't believe you," said the elf. He sighed, "I'll have to produce the evidence. I'll come up at the left ear."

Anna went to the kitchen window.

She positioned herself so that the bright morning sun shone on her ear.

"Come here," she said. "Look at the elf."

Papa stopped coughing and spluttering and came to the window with Mama. They bent over Anna's ear. It was obvious that they did not believe in the elf.

Off you go; do it now, elf, thought Anna.

She felt the ear tickle.

Mama whispered, "What's that?"

Papa whispered back, "Great God, there's something violet coming out!"

"That's his pointy cap," said Anna.

Then she felt the pricking in her outer ear. That was caused by the little elfin fingers as he clung fast to her skin.

"It's true. It's an elf," whispered Mama

"I'm cracking up," said Papa.

The elf pulled the pointy cap from his head and roared as loud as he could (but it was still very soft), "God be with you!" Then he stuck on his cap again, slid back into the ear again and disappeared.

Papa staggered to the kitchen table and slumped on the bench. Mama sat down beside him.

Anna thought: it seems to me that they've really flipped—especially Papa. He is as white as a sheet!

"Well, I tell you," said the elf, "when a mite like me survived the sight of those two giants, they surely could stand the sight of me."

For the best part of half an hour Papa and Mama sat huddled speechless together. Anna sat opposite and waited. The elf had been asleep for a long time. Mama was the first to find her voice. She cleared her throat and said, "We'll just have to live with it."

Whereupon Papa cleared *his* throat and said, "But how we can manage that I just don't know!"

Anna cried, "You don't have to do anything! You've lived already for nearly a year with the elf. You just didn't know it!"

"That's true," said Mama.

"And he will not come out of my ear again," said Anna. "It takes too much out of him. He did it that time only so that you'd believe me."

"Who apart from us knows anything about this?" asked Papa.

"No one," Anna assured them.

"Not even Peter?" asked Papa.

"Not even him," said Anna, "and I'll never mention it to another living soul."

Papa sighed with relief. In spite of her double love problems, Anna had to smile. She gave Papa a kiss on the cheek and she gave Mama a kiss on the cheek. "It won't be too bad," she whispered to Mama.

She suddenly felt herself to be big and strong. The two of them are sat there, she thought, as if all belonging to them were dead! All that has happened is that we now have an elf.

14
Anna Writes a Letter

How little one should love and still have it count as *love*, Anna still hadn't worked out by Monday morning, even though she had discussed the problem with Mama and Papa for hours on Sunday.

Mama had been of the mind that Anna needn't worry about it. "You love Hermann, anyway," she had explained. "You visited him; you went to the pictures with him. You worry about him and you think about him; that is a kind of love!"

Anna had objected: "The worrying and the thinking about Hermann is done by the elf!"

"That makes no difference," Mama had argued. "After all the elf belongs to your brain. What's inside you is *you*!"

Papa didn't take the affair very seriously. He said, Anna is a good person. And good people love all other people in some way or other. Since Hermann belongs to the class of "all other people" Anna must love him too in some way or other. Even if she isn't aware of it.

That did not satisfy Anna. It was the "some way or other" that stuck her. Whether "some way or other" was sufficient to prevent the elf from drying up and shrinking she couldn't be sure. Still she wasn't as tearfully unhappy any more as on Saturday night. It had helped greatly that Papa and Mama now knew the facts. She was again a bit hopeful that things might work out all right.

Papa thought so too. At breakfast on Monday morning he said to Anna, "You'll find that Peter isn't at all cross with you any more. Someone who loves you couldn't hold out like that."

And as Anna set off for school Papa said as she left, "Perhaps he's not cross with you at all. Maybe his sister was greatly exaggerating."

Unfortunately Peter's sister had not exaggerated at all. Peter was already in class when Anna arrived. He was surrounded by kids who were telling him what had happened at school during his absence.

Anna sat down in her place. Her heart was really pounding. Diagonally in front of her Hermann crouched, tidying his school things. He turned round to Anna. "Look," he said, "my mama has invited you to the cinema, next Saturday. In a totally fantastic one in the city centre, to see a brand new film." Oh, yes, thought Anna, his mama will bring us to a *nicer* cinema to see a *better* film. But out of consideration to the elf she smiled at Hermann in a friendly way and murmured, "Great! That's terrific."

The school buzzer went and the children who had been standing around Peter ran to their places and Peter ran up to the front to the teacher's desk. Anna heard him say to the teacher, "Please, I don't want to sit beside Anna any more. May I sit somewhere else? I don't mind where."

"That is totally out of the question," said the teacher.

"I'm not going to make a new seating arrangement every couple of weeks. You must sit beside Anna. The holidays begin a couple of weeks from now. You can surely put up with sitting beside Anna for that couple of weeks. After the holidays, in the new school year, you can see about another place."

Peter made a really horrible face as he sat down beside Anna.

"You are mean," whispered Anna.

Peter would not look at her at all.

"I've done nothing on you," whispered Anna.

Peter stared ahead at the empty blackboard.

"Why do you believe all that Michi told you?" whispered Anna.

Peter kept his eyes fixed on the blackboard and hissed to Anna, "Because it's true! Everybody says it! Maybe you didn't go to his home? Or to the pictures, eh?"

Anna was pleased that the teacher saw Peter and called, "Peter! Give over! Stop talking! You can chat at break! This is not a café!"

Anna thought, there is no way I can explain this correctly to Peter without mentioning the elf. Listen, you! Why can't I simply tell Peter about you?

"Ach, do what you want!" said the elf in a dull voice. "This business has got too much for me. I have no further advice to give you. I can't. It's every man for himself. I'm just scared that I'll end up a nit. I can't think of anything else to do."

The elf sobbed, "I'm sorry, Anna. I can't help it. It's best if I fall asleep and wait to see if I wake up as a shrunken dot. All the best, Anna."

Anna would nearly have started to sob in sympathy

with the poor elf but she gritted her teeth and bravely held back her tears. Then she thought: If Peter could see the elf only once then he'd have to believe me. Then he would love me again!

"Don't think for a moment that I'll come out again," sobbed the elf. "After all, my trips out have been simply disastrous. A person should not go against his nature. That's a piece of wisdom that I will follow from now on. Tell whoever you like about me! Tell the teacher too and the whole class! But don't count on me to provide the evidence."

Anna didn't dare to change the elf's mind. She realised that he was so deep in despair that he couldn't concern himself with her troubles. Her romance had been shattered, but what was that compared to the threatened fate of shrinking so small as to turn into a nit?

Anna sent a thought to the elf: Sleep on, poor elf. Somehow I'll manage this on my own. Just leave it to me.

Peter didn't speak to Anna at any of the breaks. Hermann was pleased. But of course he had it quite wrong. He thought that Anna didn't want to talk to Peter any more. At midday in the cloakroom he said to her, "Since you aren't going to Peter in the afternoon, you can always come with me."

"Perhaps," Anna muttered. "I'll see." She couldn't manage to be more friendly. But it was sufficient for Hermann. It pleased him so much that he blushed. And that in turn pleased Anna. She thought, he feels himself to be loved by me. Great! That's the main thing.

When Anna left the school Hermann came with her to the corner of the street. "I'll wait for your mama with you."

Anna did not refuse him. It was really boring to wait at the corner by herself.

Alma joined them too. "Hi," she said. "I belong with you. You are my friends." Then she said to Hermann, "Listen. My mama has allowed me to go home with you today. So we can so our homework together. It's much pleasanter for two to do it than one."

Hermann didn't seem all that keen but he didn't object.

At that Mama's car drove up and stopped on the other side of the street. Anna ran across the road and jumped into the car. She waved at Hermann until Mama swung round at the next intersection. Waving is a form of friendship and that is part of loving. Anna was satisfied. Because of the way I behaved to Hermann today, there's no danger that the elf will shrivel and shrink.

"How was Peter?" asked Mama anxiously.

"He's not speaking to me any more," said Anna.

"He's a twit," muttered Mama.

Anna nodded.

"But sooner or later," said Mama, "it would have happened anyway without the elf and Hermann. Possessive men always find reasons for jealousy, even where none exist."

Anna thought, that may be so but in spite of it I cannot turn off my love for Peter like a tap. And Paul and the sisters and the baby and Peter's parents, I love them too. The fact that I cannot ever see them again is nearly as bad.

As if she was a thought-reader Mama murmured, "Yeah! It's a mess!"

In Mama's flat Anna first did her homework; then she

helped Mama fill a big bag of old clothes for the Red Cross collection. Then Anna and Mama washed the tiles in the bathroom. As they worked Mama asked, "How would it be if you wrote Peter a letter?"

"What can I put in it if I can't mention the elf?" asked Anna.

"The situation must be explained without mentioning the elf," said Mama. She threw the cloth into the water, dried her hands and said, "We'll do that straight away. When it came to writing letters I was always the tops."

Mama went into her room, took her typewriter from the shelves, set in on the table, screwed a sheet of pink paper into the machine and typed, *Dear Peter.* Then she lifted her two index fingers off the keys, put them in her mouth and bit the nails. Anna sat beside her and waited. She did not dare disturb Mama when she was composing a letter.

Mama took the fingers out of her mouth and slammed them down on the keys again. Anna stared hardly breathing at the letters that the typewheel printed on the pink paper:

Since you haven't understood me I will explain everything by letter. This is how things are:

That's what I too would have written, thought Anna. But what's coming next?

Mama continued to type:

Hermann is very keen on me. Since I'm aware of that I feel it my duty to be friendly to him. Apart from me no one is nice to him. And everybody needs someone to love him. Otherwise Hermann will get a lot odder than he is already. But that has absolutely nothing to do with the great bursting love I feel for you. And if you don't believe me about that, then you're a desperate blockhead altogether and not worth the feelings I have for you!

Mama tore the pink paper out of the typewriter. "Can't you leave out the last sentence?" asked Anna.

"Why?" Mama shook her head. "The last sentence is the best, believe me!"

Mama put a fountain pen into Anna's hand. "Sign it," she said. Anna hesitated. She said, "Couldn't we at least leave out 'blockhead'?"

Mama shook her head again. "It's what he is!" she insisted. "And the truth should be told. And if I scratch out the 'blockhead' then the letter will look like begging. And you're no beggar. Or are you?"

"No!" said Anna. She unscrewed the fountain pen and wrote *Kindest regards, your Anna* at the bottom of the letter.

Mama put the letter in a pink envelope. Anna wrote Peter's address on the envelope. Then Mama and Anna took the letter to the post office. Anna breathed a kiss on the pink envelope before she put it in the box.

15
Hermann Loves Alma!

Next day at school Peter again did not speak a single word to Anna.

Anna thought, it's obvious! He hasn't got the letter yet. The postman will bring it this forenoon. He'll not be able to read it till midday.

At playtime, down in the yard, Alma asked Anna, "Hey there, Anna! Would you like to come home with me this afternoon? Hermann's coming too. I have this crazy Punch and Judy theatre. Then two of us can do the acting and the other will be the audience!"

However, Anna had no time for Punch and Judy. She had to go with Mama to the dentist. Mama had a large cavity in a back tooth, bottom right. And Mama had a phobia about the dentist. She couldn't manage a visit to the dentist without Anna. Otherwise she'd simply turn at the dentist's door and head for home again.

So Anna had a dentist-afternoon. Not that the dentist would have been drilling for the whole afternoon in Mama's mouth. No, but first Mama quaked with sheer dental terror and Anna had to give her a good talking-to. Then they went by taxi to the surgery. "I'm so nervous," said Mama, "that I couldn't possibly steer a car. I'd be sure to drive clear through a red light and end up wrapped round the next lamppost.

Then Anna sat beside her mother for an hour in the dentist's waiting-room and tried to unhook her from her phobia. She made Mama look at magazines with her.

When Mama's turn came, she wanted to let the man who had been sitting beside her waiting, go in front of her. "I'm in no hurry," she said to him.

The man was in no hurry either and declined Mama's offer. He clearly had dentist phobia too.

"Now I'll take you in, Mama," said Anna. "We'll go together." She pulled Mama off her chair and bundled her into the surgery.

While the dentist was drilling, Anna held her mother's hand. The dentist laughed about it. "This is a topsy-turvy world where the children stay with the mothers and have to do the consoling."

After the visit to the dentist Mama was so shaken that she had to have a rest. Anna went with Mama, again in a taxi, to Papa's apartment. She lay down in the living-room on the sofa, while Anna did her homework. She had to write ten sentences. Since the dwarf wasn't awake Anna's work went a bit askew. She made ten mistakes in ten sentences. Three times she wrote a proper noun with a small letter, twice she wrote a verb with a capital letter, three times she forgot a silent "h" and twice she wrote "ei" instead of "ie."

Mama checked the homework but she was so zonked that she did not notice a single mistake. Papa discovered the ten errors that evening when he was helping Anna to tidy her schoolbag. By then Mama had gone home.

Papa used ink-remover on the homework and

corrected the ten mistakes very smartly.

"You are a very nice papa," she said in praise.

"And you are a very nice daughter," said Papa.

Then Papa and Anna watched the telly for a bit and afterwards shared a foam bath and washed each other's hair. During the hairwashing Anna told Papa about the letter that Mama had written in her name. Papa considered the letter a great idea. And what Mama had written pleased him too. "When Peter reads that," he said, "he's bound to be nice to you again."

Anna said nothing to Papa about the elf. She had noticed that Papa didn't want that. She had a suspicion that Papa would much prefer to forget the elf.

Next morning Anna was the first pupil in the classroom. Not even the teacher was there. She still sat below in the staffroom.

Anna sat down in her desk. She was so excited that her hands shook. As she took out her school stuff her hands shook so much that erasers and coloured pencils fell on the floor.

Slowly the classroom filled up. There was a lot of noisy chat around Anna. Alma came over to Anna and told her that she and Hermann had had a smashing afternoon playing with the Punch and Judy show. "Once there was a bit of a punch-up," she said, "because Hermann was acting the gipe, but apart from that it was magic!"

And when Hermann came along he too told Anna that the afternoon had been "magic." "Alma is great crack," he said, "and she knows millions of jokes. And she knows three very rude songs as well. When she sings you crease yourself laughing. This afternoon Alma's coming to my house. Are you coming too?"

"I'm not sure yet," said Anna. "My mama is collecting me. I'll have to ask her if she'll allow me."

Hermann didn't seem to be disappointed at Anna's answer. "Well, if today's no good," he said, "then be sure to come tomorrow. By the way, I'll always be with Alma in the afternoons from now on. I have to help her with her homework, you see. In the Tyrol, where she was for so long, they were learning a lot of different stuff. She's quite far behind in a whole lot of things."

Peter didn't arrive into the classroom until the bell was ringing. He sat beside Anna, shoved his schoolbag into the desk, lifted the letter which Anna had written him and dropped it in Anna's lap.

The letter was still sealed. Peter had written in felt pen on the envelope in huge red letters: *Delivery refused*!

Anna put the letter in her pink satchel and thought: this isn't happening! This can't be true! He hasn't even read my letter! And this is supposed to be love! Only a genuine blockhead loves like that!

Anna got blazingly angry. There was no longer a place for sadness in her head. For the whole morning she was red-hot with anger. And she found that just great. Anger doesn't make you feel as unhappy as sadness. You can fling the rubber at the desk so hard that it bounces nearly to the ceiling and press so heavily with a ballpoint on the exercise page that the paper is torn to shreds. At playtime Anna sat alone below in the yard on the seat by the lilac bush and scrabbled her heels in the gravel until the dust whirled about her. And all the while she muttered, "Blockhead, blockhead, stupid stupid stupid blockhead!"

When playtime was over and Anna got up from the

bench there were two deep holes in the ground and Anna's heels were badly worn down. The rubber soles were in flitters. And the red-hot anger was gone.

Anna decided that in the afternoon she would do something for the poor elf. She thought, I will go to Hermann and be his love.

However, when Anna went into the cloakroom to tell Hermann, he had already gone.

"He went straight out with Alma," said Susi. "They're absolutely crazy about each other."

Anna ran to the school gate. She saw Hermann and Alma heading for the intersection. Hermann had a schoolbag in each hand—in his right his own bag and in the left Alma's.

"Hey, wait for me," cried Anna and she ran to the intersection. However, when she got there the pedestrian crossing light was at red and Hermann and Alma were already on the other side of the street. "Hello, Hermann!" shouted Anna and waved. Hermann and Alma didn't hear her. The two of them were standing in front of the window of a toyshop looking at stuffed animals. Hermann had put down the two schoolbags and had his arm round Alma's shoulders.

Anna let her arm fall to her side and thought: this changes the situation entirely.

"I believe so, too," said the elf. His voice sounded happy.

How long have you been awake? thought Anna.

"Your red-hot anger woke me," said the elf. "It got so hot inside your skull that I have been soaked with sweat."

"And how do you feel?" asked Anna anxiously.

"Perfect," said the elf. "Fit and well as ever I was! The nit danger seems to have been removed." The elf giggled. "I find it splendid," said he, "that Herr Mann had done my work for me. He has laid the conduit from *Love* to *Alma* himself!"

It's gotta be right, thought Anna.

"And so," said the elf, "you don't need to torture yourself about Herr Mann again: he loves Alma; Alma loves him. That's sufficient. To be loved by two girls would be a luxury!"

Exactly, thought Anna. Especially when it was fiendishly difficult for one of the two girls!

Mama's car came driving up the street and stopped beside Anna. She got in.

"Well?" said Mama.

Anna opened her satchel, took out the letter and gave it to her Mama.

"Such cheek!" cried Mama. "That blockhead needs a walloping!" She drew Anna close. "Are you very sad, treasure?"

Anna shook her head.

"Really not?" Mama seemed not to believe it.

"I was terribly angry," said Anna. "But that has died down too. She lifted one leg high and put it on the arm of the passenger seat. "Look, Mama." Anna pointed to the heel of her shoe. "In sheer anger I wrecked my shoes."

Mama looked in astonishment at the worn-down heels and the tatters of rubber sole that hung from them.

"The other one looks just the same," said Anna.

"How did you manage to do that?" asked Mama.

"I scraped off my anger in the gravel," said Anna.

"What a good idea!" said Mama. "I must remember

that for future reference."

Then Mama and Anna drove to the nearest shoe-shop and bought new sandals for Anna, red-strapped ones with sparklers on the straps.

Mama bought herself sandals as well, white ones with very high heels.

"Now," said Mama after the double purchase, "I have spent all my cash." She rooted in her purse. "What's in here wouldn't stretch to pizzas in a restaurant."

"Well," asked Anna, "what would it stretch to?"

"To four yeast pastries and two Cokes," said Mama. So she and Anna went into a cake-shop and bought four pastries and two Cokes. They found seats in the park and ate the pastries and drank the Cokes.

Mama held her face up to the sun and asked, "How is the elf?"

"In great form again," said Anna, and she told Mama about the new love between Hermann and Alma.

"Crazy," said Mama. Then she asked, "Is he fast asleep or is he awake?"

"I'm about to fall asleep," whispered the elf and yawned.

"He's about to fall asleep," said Anna.

Mama bent forward towards Anna and whispered in her ear, "Sleep well, my dear elf."

Anna leant her head on Mama's shoulder. "Y'know," said she, "Papa isn't in tune with my elf. To Papa he's a bit scary, I think."

"That could be," said Mama. "Don't ever talk to him about the elf. It'll be enough that you can talk to me about him."

"And you don't find him scary?" asked Anna.

"Not at all!" Mama shook her head. "I'm just a little envious that I haven't one in *my* head."

16
Peter's Secret

For a whole week Peter didn't utter a single word to Anna. On the first day he didn't once look at her.

He stared obstinately at the blackboard and the elf groused, "The blockhead will end up with a real stiff neck."

On the second day, Peter darted the odd poisonous look at Anna and the elf complained, "The blockhead has something wrong with his eyes if he takes you for some kind of nasty spider."

On the third day Peter stared fixedly at Hermann and Alma. Slowly it came to him that the two were sweethearts and that Hermann spoke far more often to Alma than to Anna, and the elf growled, "Now the blockhead doesn't understand the world any more."

On the fourth day Peter kept squinting at Anna both during lessons and at the breaks and the elf jeered, "The blockhead would love to make contact with us again but he doesn't know how to go about it!"

On the last schoolday of the week, as Anna played rubber-band hopscotch with Susi down in the yard, Peter approached her. A couple of times he opened his mouth as if to say something, then closed it again.

Anna thought: he wants to be my friend again! She wanted to smile encouragingly at him but the elf roared, "Hey! Don't be an eejit. Let the blockhead stew a bit in his own juice."

Right on, thought Anna and did not smile.

On Sunday evening the phone rang in Papa's flat. Papa and Anna had just come home. They had been swimming with Mama. Papa lifted the receiver. "It's for you," he said and handed it over to Anna. "It's Peter," he whispered.

Anna took the receiver. "Yes?" she said.

"Hey, Anna," said Peter, "could you give me the letter again tomorrow in school? I'd love to read it."

"I've thrown the letter away," lied Anna. The letter lay on her desk under the paperweight. Anna did not want him to have it any more. In the letter there was something about "great love" and Anna wasn't all that certain whether that was still right.

"Couldn't you write me the letter again?" asked Peter.

"That'll be the day, you blockhead," growled the elf, and Anna, without actually wanting to, repeated after the elf, "That'll be the day, you blockhead!"

Peter murmured, "Excuse me," and put the phone down.

You cheeky thing, thought Anna grumpily, you are always pushing your opinions on to me. I did not want to say that.

"Pardon," muttered the elf. "From now on I'll hold back and not interfere again!"

And that's exactly what he did. Neither on Monday nor on Tuesday did he make any comment about Peter even though he had groused and growled about all kinds of things about him before that. Peter slumped beside Anna like a terminally ill kid. He was pale; his eyes were dead in his head; he spoke to no one; he stayed in his seat during the breaks. He didn't eat his snack either and when the teacher asked him anything he answered in such a weak voice that she didn't understand him and had to repeat the question.

Anna thought: if he were to ask me now to be his friend again, I'd say yes.

Not once did the elf break into speech. Anyway Peter didn't ask. However, he was *silently* friendly to Anna. When Anna had written her fountain pen dry and had no more cartridges in her pencil-case, Peter took his reserve cartridge out of his pen and pushed it across to her. When Anna wanted to rub out a line in her drawing and her hard eraser left dirty marks on the paper, Peter handed her his soft rubber. And at every break Peter took a sweet out of his schoolbag and left it on Anna's half of the desk. Anna ate the sweet and was very touched.

On Wednesday evening, as Anna was getting out of Mama's car in front of Papa's flat, there stood one of Peter's big sisters in the doorway. "I've been waiting for you," said she to Anna, "because I must speak to you. Because it can't go on. Because Peter is ill with lovesickness."

The big sister went into the house with Anna and up the stairs. "Peter is really cracking up," she said. "He's falling to pieces on us!"

The big sister looked really worried. "Do you know what he told me yesterday in the midst of howling and sobbing?"

"No," said Anna.

"But don't let it go any further," she said. "Because no one should get to hear of this."

"Not at all," said Anna.

The big sister stopped in the middle of the flight of stairs. She bent forward and whispered in Anna's ear, "He insists that he's not to blame for his stupid jealousy. An elf with a yellow peaked cap is responsible. He lives in Peter's head. And makes him say things."

"Great heavens," shrieked the elf. "A yellow! Yellows are wacky!"

Anna didn't know what to say to the big sister. She stayed quiet and climbed on up the stairs. The big sister took Anna's silence for dismay. She climbed up after Anna and said, "But I'm sure that his craziness would disappear if you were nice to him!"

When they got to the door of the flat, Anna dug the key-ring out of the front of her T-shirt and opened it. Papa stood in the hallway. "So you've brought a visitor?" he asked.

"No," said the big sister. "I'm going. I just had to tell Anna something." Then she whispered to Anna, "So not a word to anyone. Please!" And she ran down the stairs.

Papa's eyes blazed with curiosity. "What did she want?"

"Just an elf problem," said Anna. At that Papa disappeared into the kitchen like greased lightning. He wanted no truck with elf problems. Anna went into the kitchen too, sat down on the corner bench, looked at Papa as he prepared supper and quizzed the elf: Why are the yellow caps so crazy?

The elf said, "Why they are crazy, I don't know. But that they are completely bonkers is well known to our lot. At any rate they have a tendency to spread mistrust and suspicion in any heads where they are living!"

Anna asked the elf, what if I talked to him? What if I talked to him nicely. In through Peter's ear?

At first the elf didn't answer. It was only when Anna thought, hey there! What's up? I asked you a question, that the elf said, "They are as stubborn as goats! They won't pay the slightest attention to someone like you." Then he stopped speaking again.

Anna realised that he was giving the matter some thought. She knew her dwarf after all. She waited patiently until the elf spoke again. "You have to talk to a yellow in our own language," he said. "Our lot are bilingual. We are fluent in both Human and Elf!"

How does Elf sound? Anna wanted to know.

"For you it has no sound at all," said the elf. "We manage to communicate soundlessly. It flashes like electricity from brain to brain but only between those close together. Elf doesn't reach far."

How far? asked Anna.

"About the thickness of a little finger," said the elf.

Anna stood up. "Can you postpone supper for about an hour?" she asked Papa. "I've got to go off again."

"To see Peter?" asked Papa

Anna nodded.

"Cross at the lights," said Papa.

Anna nodded.

"Good luck, Anna," called Papa after her as she ran out of the flat.

Peter's mama opened the door for her. "I've missed you terribly," she said

"And I you," said Anna. She went to the living-room. Peter's papa lay on the sofa. He had the baby on his stomach. The baby spat the dummy out and smiled at Anna and Peter's father yelled, "It's great that you're back."

The big sister who had visited Anna sat at the dinner table painting her nails and winked at her. The other big sister came out of the sisters' bedroom. "Ah, our Anna," she cried. "All the misery is over." She pointed to Peter and Paul's room. "Paul is visiting a friend. Go on in. You won't be disturbed."

Peter stood at the window looking out, exactly as if he hadn't heard that Anna had come. And of course he must have heard. Through the thin walls of Peter's flat you could hear every word. Anna went over to Peter. She took him by the hand and led him to the bunk bed. She sat down on the edge of the lower bed. Peter sat down beside her. She snuggled very close to Peter and leant her head against Peter's so that her left ear was touching his right.

"As a matter of fact I have one with a violet cap," said

she, "and he wants to talk to yours. In Elf-Electric that we can't hear."

For a long time Peter and Anna sat there. Ear to ear. So as not to disturb the elves. They held each other's hand tightly. Nothing in fact was to be heard from the elves. Anna just felt a gentle tingle in her ear. Then the tingling stopped and she knew by the light tickle that the elf had slid into her ear again. Immediately he said, "The yellow wants to beg humble pardon. He has realised that he has done you wrong!"

Anna nodded and drew back a little from Peter so that she could look at his face. Peter had his eyes closed. Anna thought, he's talking to his elf!

Then he opened his eyes and said to Anna, "He swears that he won't put any more nonsense into my head. But he has often made a promise and not kept it."

"Mine often acts crazily too," said Anna, "but when I fight with him he always gives in in the end."

"I'll just not listen to him ever again," said Peter. He snuggled again very close to Anna and put his face against hers. Ear by ear they sat there. But there was no more tingling in the ears.

"Mine's certainly asleep already," said Peter. "He needs lots of sleep."

"Mine too," said Anna.

So Peter and Anna sat there until Peter's mama knocked at the room door and called, "Apricot dumplings! If you don't came soon they'll all be gone."

Then Peter and Anna jumped up and ran, hand in hand, into the living-room. There were still ten dumplings left. These Peter and Anna ate up.

They shared every one. Peter ate one half of each

dumpling and Anna ate the other. In the same way they drank apple juice out of the same glass, mouth by mouth.

After supper the whole of Peter's family left Anna home. Even Peter's papa went with them although his legs were very tired. And Anna was allowed to push the baby in the buggy.

At the corner before Papa's house they met a woman who greeted Peter's mama and stood and said, "Hello. I thought that you had only five kids. But you have six."

With a perfectly serious face Peter's mama answered, "Yes. We have six; it would be a pity to have only five." As soon as the woman had gone and could no longer hear, they all began to laugh and they kept laughing until they reached the entrance to Papa's house.

Papa stood at the open window of the living-room and waved at Anna. Anna and Peter, the big sisters, Paul, the baby and Peter's parents waved back.

Anna said to Peter, "When you come on Sunday with Mama and Papa and me to the Prater, all the people will believe that my parents have two kids."

Then Anna ran into the house and raced up the stairs. Papa stood in the open door of the flat. "Everything okay?" he asked.

"Completely okay," puffed Anna. "I'm the sixth child of Peter's parents and Peter is the second child of you and Mama."

"So there are two extra children in the world," murmured Papa.

"The guy's arithmetic is wrong, isn't it?" asked the elf.

Anna thought, in one way yes, but in another, no.

"That's too complicated for me," said the elf and yawned, loud and clear. And three times in succession.

Anna yawned too loud and clear. And three times after each other.

"Sure," said Papa. "Happiness is tiring."

"Then I'm the happiest elf in the world," murmured the elf and began to snore loudly.

Tex and Sheelagh

By

Gordon Snell

Tex and Sheelagh are two very smart kittens who come to live with writers Dick and Moira and have great fun exploring the world of humans. A fierce dog called Wolf lives nearby but they soon make friends with him and with the other cats of the neighbourhood.

Then one night, intruders arrive when Dick and Moira are out of the house. What can the kittens do to help their owners whom they have grown to love?

Tarantula!

By

Rose Doyle

Ben is ten and Bobby is nine. Life at home has been miserable for them since their baby sister arrived. They decide to stow away on a ship to Liverpool to visit their Uncle John, a cool dude who will surely give them the holiday of their lives.

In a warehouse in the Dublin docks they meet Zaby, a Nigerian girl who has stowed away in the opposite direction. Then Murt arrives. He is a drug smuggler, a nasty piece of work, and he doesn't let anything or anybody stand in his way—except maybe large tropical spiders...

Tarantula! is a really gripping yarn, full of hair-raising suspense.

The Boy Who Saved Christmas

By
Vincent McDonnell

Why should Christmas need to be saved? Because it is in real danger of being lost!

Not many people knew it: it was all hushed up, of course. Santa Claus was kidnapped by the vilest gang of crooks that ever lived. The bravery and intelligence of computerwise Timmy Goodfellow and his animal friends are sorely needed, otherwise Christmas might disappear—for ever!

Vincent McDonnell was the recipient of the GPA First Fiction award in 1989. This is his first book for children.

A Monster Called Charlie

By

Margrit Cruickshank

Daniel opened the front door. And there on the mat stood a monster.

It wasn't a big monster. It wasn't a huge scaly monster that breathed fire at you. Or a big hairy monster that could crush you with one paw tied behind its back. In fact, it was really quite small. It had a fat furry, green tummy, a small snouty head, big black eyes with long blue eyelashes, two stumpy scaly wings and a short fat scaly tail.

Daniel has always wanted a monster for a friend but he didn't expect it to cause so much trouble. As Charlie discovers how *not* to deal with life on Earth, Daniel and his sister Kate begin to wonder if taking in a space monster was such a good idea.

Margrit Cruickshank was shortlisted for the Irish Book Awards in 1990 and in 1992 for the Bisto Book of the Year Award.